UNDERSTANDING MUSIC

Robert L. Reid

illustrated by
William Reid

Revised Edition

J. Weston Walch, Publisher
Portland, Maine

1 2 3 4 5 6 7 8 9 10
ISBN 0-8251-1731-3

J. Weston Walch, Publisher
P.O. Box 658 • Portland, Maine 04104-0658

Printed in the United States of America

Contents

Introduction

There is an entertaining game called "Trivia" which all of us have played at one time or another. Someone chooses a subject and then the players try to stump each other by asking the most obscure questions they can think of relating to the chosen subject. Sometimes the subject is the movies: Which film won the Academy Award for Best Picture in 1963? Sometimes it is baseball: Who holds the record for the most stolen bases in a single season?

Often the game starts when an old popular song is played on the radio. Players grow silent and start shuffling through the music files in their brains, trying to be the first to identify the piece. Finally someone shouts, "That's Little Richard and he's singing 'Long Tall Sally'!"

You may have noticed that some people are better than others at playing musical trivia. They seem to have the ability to recall sounds and lyrics without really trying. If they like classical music, they can hear just a few seconds of a piece and announce immediately, "Easy! It's Beethoven's *Fifth Symphony.*" Or if they are interested in rock music, they can listen to a song for a moment and then say, "That's the Stones' 'Gimme Shelter.' "

These people can recall specific sounds quickly. They can relate them to the names of performers and songs. But you might ask yourself: Do they really *understand* music? Or are they like someone who knows the Latin names for every flower in the garden, but doesn't see their beauty? In other words, is it possible that experts at musical trivia are missing something?

The answer is that if all they can do is supply names and song titles, such people are indeed missing something. They understand music only partially. In their favor is the fact that they have a feeling for the history of music. Certainly this is important for a full understanding of what music is all about. Even though they may not know exactly which piece is being played, they can relate it to other works they have heard, placing it before some works and after others simply by virtue of the sound of the piece to which they are listening. By a process of elimination, they can help themselves to identify the piece.

But there is more to understanding music than simply understanding music history. And it is in these other areas where musical trivia experts sometimes fail. The purpose of this book is to introduce you to some of these other areas. Familiarity with each of them will bring you closer to an understanding of what music is all about.

This, then, is not a book about music history. Instead, it is a book about the ingredients that go into a piece of music to make it what it is. Those ingredients don't change. We will see that what was true for a symphony written 200 years ago can also be true for a contemporary popular song. And we will find that the elements of music do not depend upon what kind of music is being played. String quartets and folk songs, concertos and rock music, jazz and sonatas—all have certain basic components in common. Our objective will be to find just what it is that goes into music which gives it that life we all find so appealing. If we can understand what is inside music, then perhaps we can understand music itself.

To familiarize yourself with the principal periods and styles of music history, study the charts which follow. Obviously, charts of this nature cannot be complete. They are meant only to give a very general idea of some of the important movements in music history. The charts also list a few of music's most important composers and performers. Since this is not a history book, you won't be expected to learn the information contained on the charts, but you will find it helpful to gain at least an elementary familiarity with the areas of music which are listed. You may be startled to find that there are so many of them to learn about. Perhaps you would find it interesting to pick one or two specific areas to study on your own.

But remember—to understand music, you should understand what goes into it. History alone, for you or for the trivia expert, is not enough.

* * * * *

Music is timeless but books about music are not. *Understanding Music* has enjoyed a long and happy life since 1972, but after seventeen years it seemed prudent to update the book to incorporate changes which have occurred during that time. Some of the changes have been technological, so I've added material to Chapter 5 to reflect the increased importance of electronics in music. I've added a new chapter that looks at how music is created and performed, and a second that discusses "new music," a topic that barely existed in 1972. The emphasis on Western music remains the same throughout the book, but I've used the subject of new music as a springboard to encourage students to move on, to explore the music of other cultures. My aim today remains the same as it was seventeen years ago, to illuminate the elements common to all types of music in an effort to further understand each.

Robert L. Reid
Albuquerque, NM
1989

Composers and Periods of Music History: Before 1800

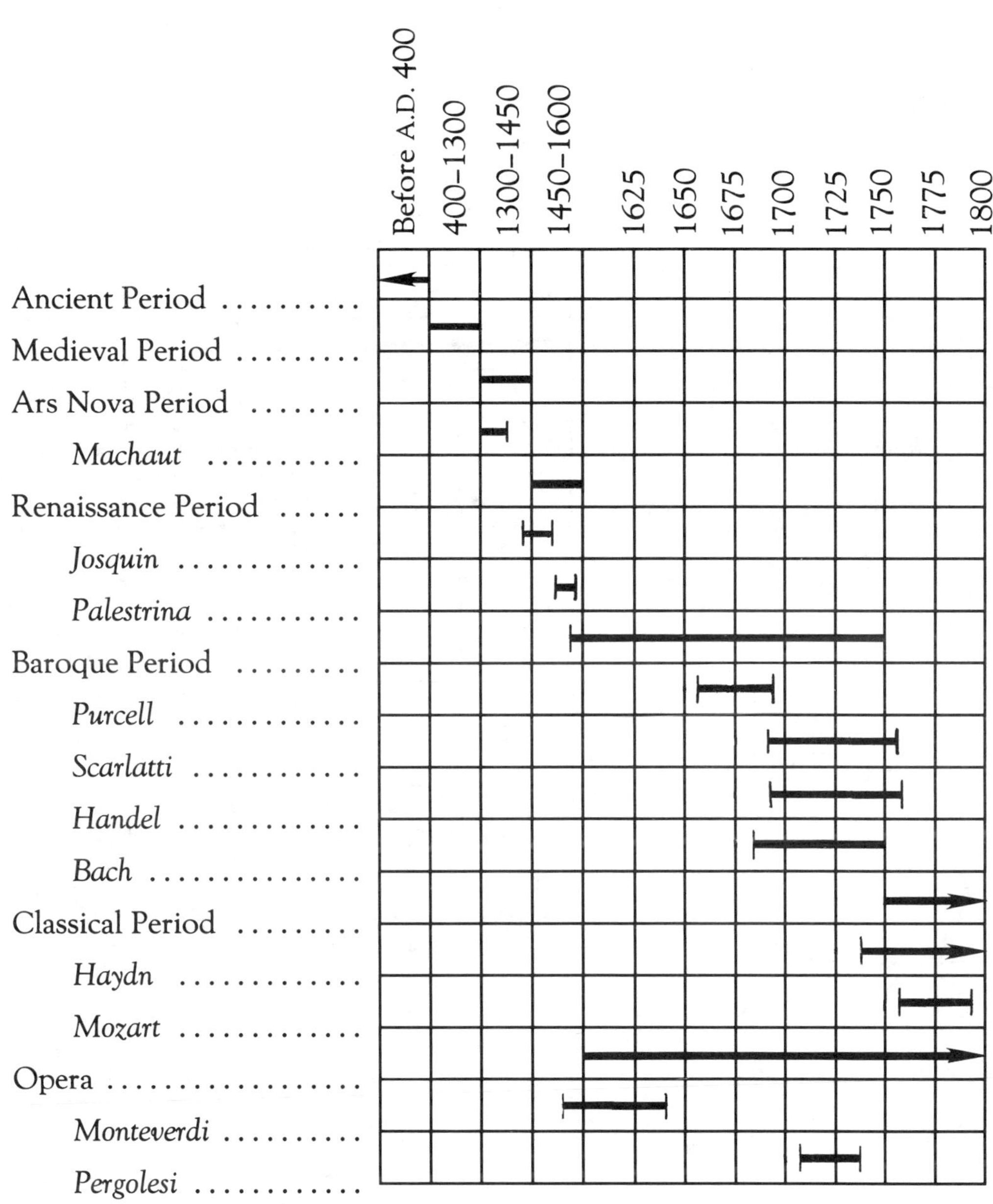

Composers and Periods of Music History: 1800–1900

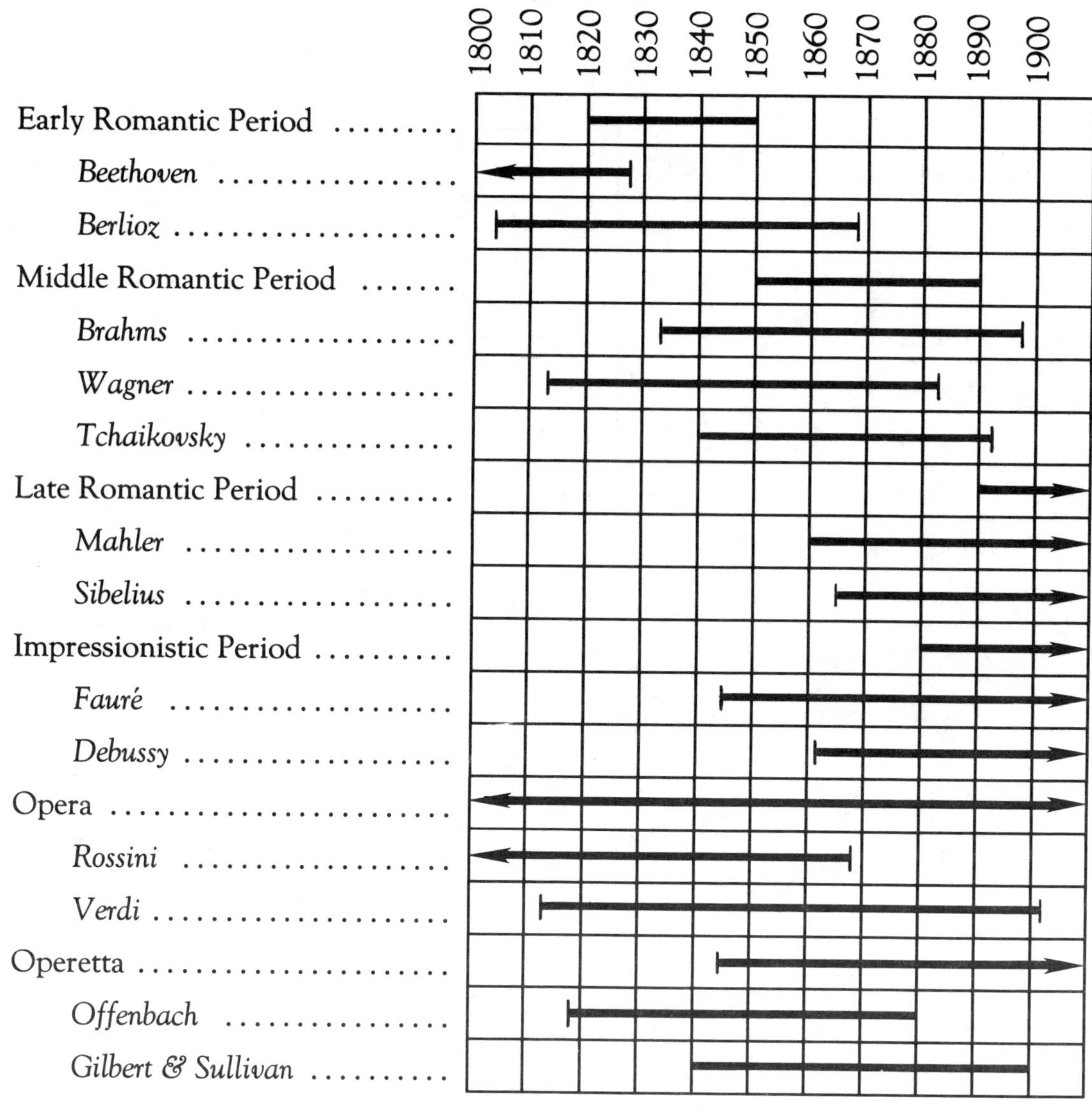

Composers and Periods of Music History: 1900–Present

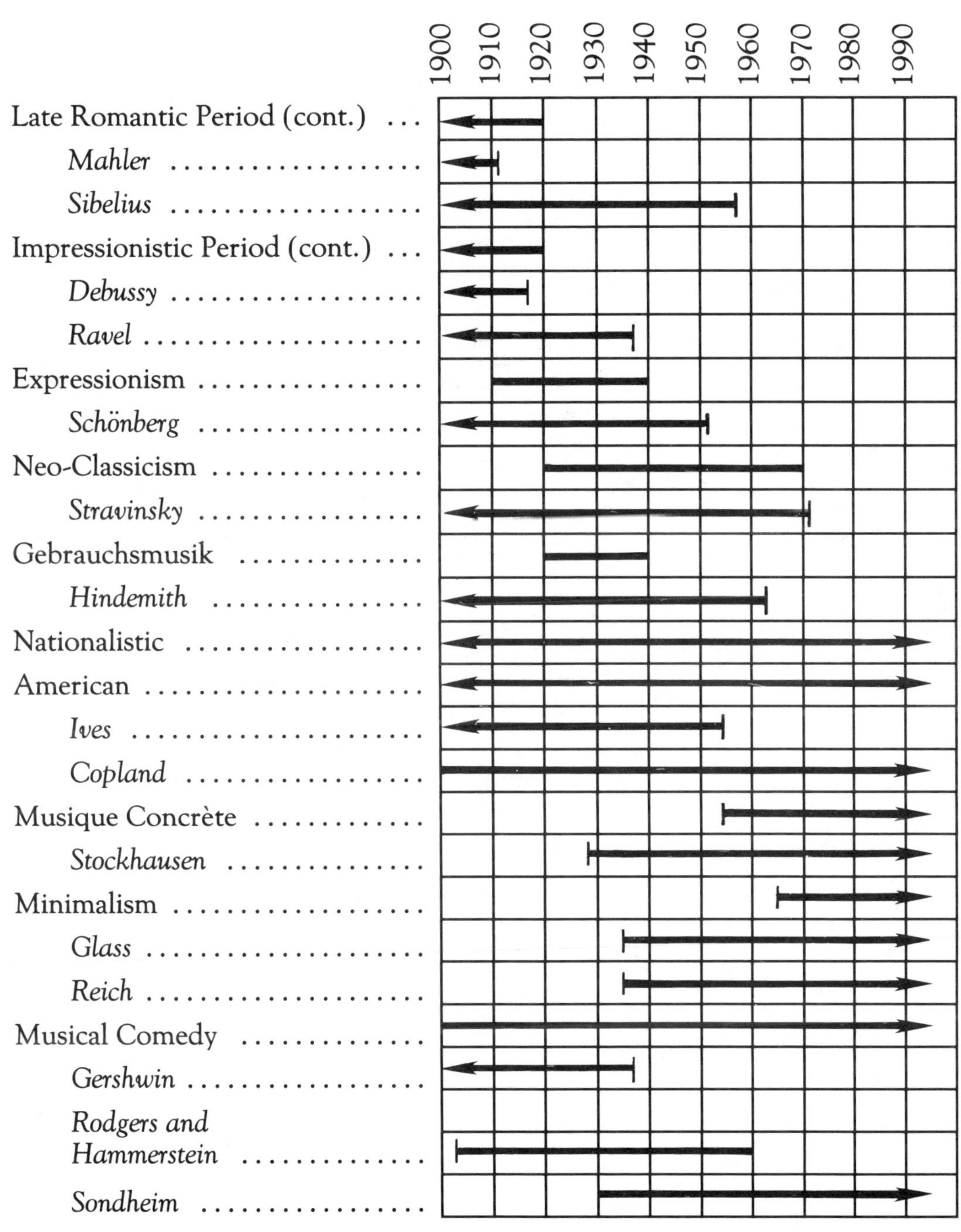

Performers and Styles of Popular Music: 1900–Present

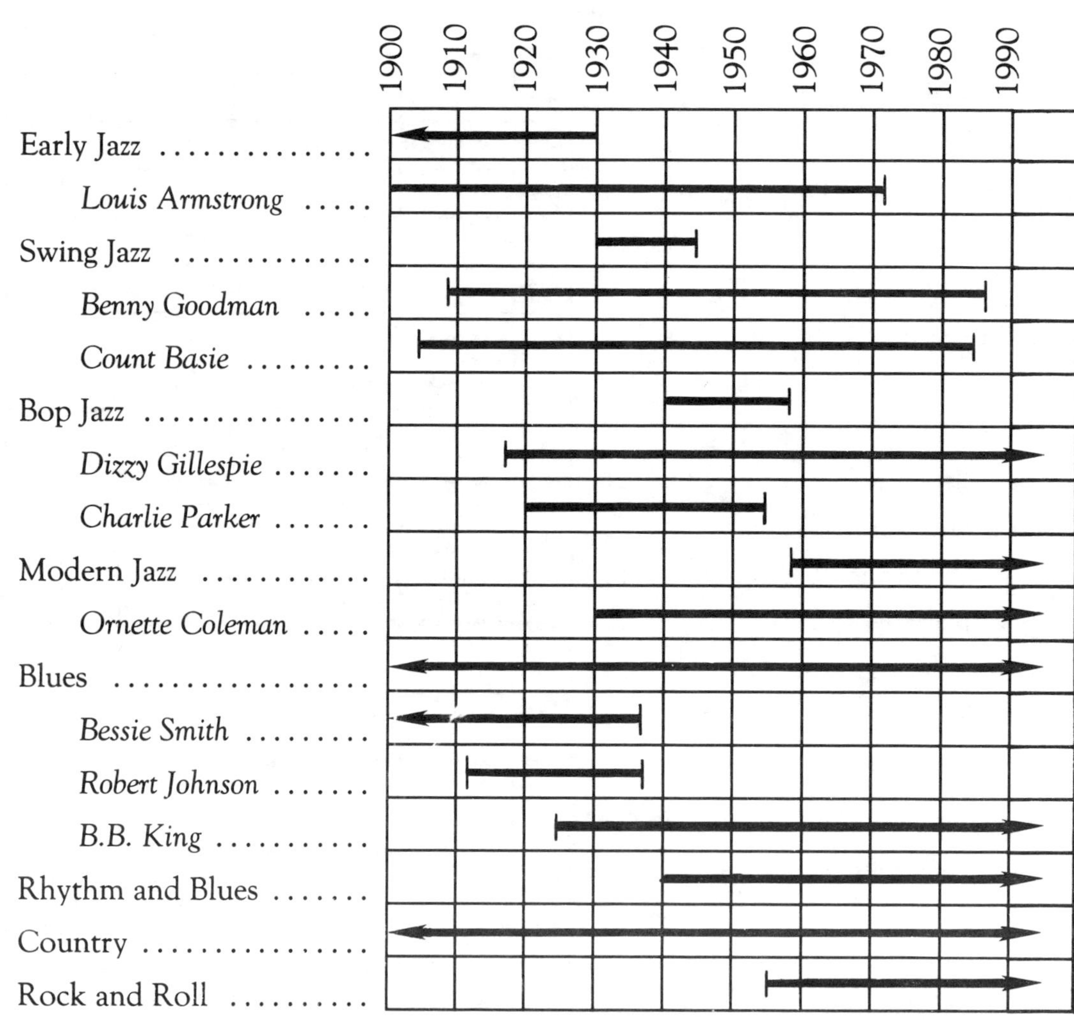

Listening List

Following is a list of the musical works referred to in this text.

Chapter 2

Schubert, *Eighth Symphony* (First Movement)
The Beatles, *Abbey Road* ("Golden Slumbers," by Paul McCartney)
Beethoven, *Third Symphony* (First Movement)
Stravinsky, *The Rite of Spring (Le Sacre du Printemps)*
The Beatles, *Abbey Road* ("Come Together," by John Lennon)

Jazz performances -
It is suggested that for contrast, an early jazz work be played, followed by a contemporary work. Recommended performers of early jazz include:

Louis Armstrong and his Hot Five
Bix Beiderbecke
Jack Teagarden
Johnny Hodges (early recordings)
Coleman Hawkins (early recordings)

Recommended performers of contemporary jazz include:

Ornette Coleman
John Coltrane
Thelonius Monk
Cecil Taylor
Sonny Rollins

Chapter 3

Chopin, *Prelude in C Minor* (for piano)
Ragtime composition -
Avoid "commercial" compositions by popular music composers such as Irving Berlin. True ragtime works were written for solo piano only. Recommended composers include:

Scott Joplin (his "Maple Leaf Rag" is a ragtime classic)
Joseph Lamb
James Scott

Strauss waltz; for example, "On the Beautiful Blue Danube," "Tales from the Vienna Woods," or "The Emperor Waltz"
Dave Brubeck Quartet, *Time Out* ("Take Five," by Paul Desmond)
Copland, *El Salón Mêxico*

Chapter 4

Wagner, *Tristan und Isolde* (Prelude)
Debussy, *La Cathédrale Engloutie* (for piano)

Modern classical composition -
Recommended composers of non-electronic music include:
Elliott Carter
David Diamond
Henry Cowell
Wallingford Riegger

Recommended composers of electronic and experimental tape-recorded music include:
Pierre Boulez
Karlheinz Stockhausen

Dvořák, *Ninth Symphony* ("New World") (Second Movement)
Meredith Willson, *The Music Man* ("Lida Rose")
Bach, *Brandenburg Concerto No. 2* (Second Movement)

Chapter 5

Britten, *The Young Person's Guide to the Orchestra*

Chapter 6

Blues composition -
Recommended performers include:
Robert Johnson
Big Bill Broonzy
Bessie Smith
Muddy Waters
John Lee Hooker
Blind Lemon Jefferson

Rachmaninoff, *Rhapsody on a Theme of Paganini*
Brahms, *Variations on a Theme by Haydn*

Charlie Parker solo -
Recommended albums include:
Greatest Recording Session (Savoy Records)
Bird at St. Nick's (Fantasy Records)
Bird & Diz (Verve Records)

Lennon-McCartney, "Hey, Jude"
Haydn, *Symphony No. 92* ("The Oxford") (Third Movement)
Haydn, *Symphony No. 94* ("The Surprise") (Third Movement)
Mozart, *Symphony No. 41* ("The Jupiter") (Third Movement)
Mozart, *Eine Kleine Nachtmusik* (Third Movement)
Beethoven, *Pathétique Sonata* (Third Movement)
Beethoven, "Archduke" *Trio* (First Movement)

Chapter 7

Tchaikovsky, *1812 Overture*
Berlioz, *Symphonie Fantastique*
Honegger, *Pacific 231*
Sibelius, *Finlandia*

Chapter 8

Solo
J.S. Bach, *The Well-Tempered Clavier*
Beethoven, *Sonatas* (Piano)
Chopin, *Nocturnes* (Piano)
Debussy, *Preludes* (Piano)
Joplin, *Rags* (Piano)
Liszt, *Hungarian Rhapsodies* (Piano)

Jazz soloists: Earl Hines (Piano)
Thelonius Monk (Piano)
Sonny Rollins (Tenor saxophone)
Art Tatum (Piano)

Duets
Beethoven, *Sonatas* (Violin and piano)
Mozart, *Sonatas* (Piano and violin)
Schubert, *Songs* (Voice and piano)

Trios

- Beethoven, The "Archduke" *Trio* and The "Ghost" Trio
- Brahms, *Piano Trios*
- Schubert, *Trio, Opus* 99

Quartets

- Beethoven, *String Quartets*
- Bartok, *String Quartets*
- Brahms, *Piano Quartets*
- Ravel, *String Quartet*

Small Jazz Groups

- Modern Jazz Quartet
- Groups led by: Louis Armstrong
  - Ornette Coleman
  - John Coltrane
  - Miles Davis
  - Dizzy Gillespie
  - Billie Holiday
  - Charles Mingus
  - Charlie Parker

Concertos

- Beethoven (Piano)
- Gershwin (Piano)
- Mendelssohn (Violin)
- Mozart (Piano and violin)
- Prokofiev (Piano)
- Shostakovich (Violin)
- Sibelius (Violin)
- Tchaikovsky (Piano and violin)

Symphonies

- Beethoven
- Brahms

Dvořák

- Mahler
- Williams
- Shostakovich
- Stravinsky

Other symphonic works
- Copland, *Appalachian Spring*
- Gershwin, *An American in Paris*
- Mussorgsky, *Pictures at an Exhibition*
- Respighi, *The Pines of Rome* and *The Fountains of Rome*
- Stravinsky, *The Firebird* and *Petrouchka*

Choral works
- Brahms, *Requiem*
- Handel, *Oratorios*
- Mahler, *Das Lied von der Erde*

Jazz Orchestras
- Duke Ellington
- Count Basie

Chapter 9

Schönberg *String Quartet in D Minor*
Five Piano Pieces

Webern

Hovhaness, *Khaldis Concerto for Piano, Four Trumpets, and Percussion*
Lousadzak Concerto for Piano and Strings
Talin

Crumb, *Haunted Landscape*

Harrison, *Three Pieces for Gamelan*
Double Concerto for Violin, Cello, and Javanese Gamelan
At the Tomb of Charles Ives

Partch

Varese, *Deserts*

Stockhausen, *Gesang der Junglinge*
Mikrophonie I
Mikrophonie II
Opus 1970

Luening-Ussachevsky, *Rhapsodic Variations*
Poem for Cycles and Bells
Concerted Piece for Tape Recorder and Orchestra

Lucier, *I Am Sitting in a Room*

Riley, *Music for the Gift*
In C

Reich, *Gonna Rain*
Come Out
Sextet
Six Marimbas
Drumming
Four Organs

Xolotl, *Last Wave*
Procession

Carlos, *Sonic Seasonings*
Digital Moonscapes

Erb, *In No Strange Land*

Glass, *Strung Out*
Glassworks
Dance 1 and 3
Company

Jazz Performers: Miles Davis
Modern Jazz Quartet
Stan Getz
Wynton Marsalis
Art Blakey
Horace Silver
Ornette Coleman
Archie Shepp
John Coltrane
Cecil Taylor
Albert Ayler
Don Cherry

Chapter 1

LISTENING

Enjoying the Fine Arts

We humans have spent the past few thousand years inventing objects and institutions designed to make ourselves more civilized beings. The results of our efforts, most people would agree, have been mixed. Some would argue that the invention of the atomic bomb was a step backward for civilization. Few would disagree that the printing press, polio vaccine, and representative government have been giant steps forward.

Among the greatest of our inventions have been the fine arts—painting, music, drama, sculpture, literature, poetry, and dance. They share a common reason for existing: the desire within each of us to create, first within ourselves and then for others, objects of great imagination without regard for their usefulness.

But despite this common reason for existing, there is a special difference between music and the other arts. Interestingly, it is this difference which leads to a common difficulty in learning to understand music. To get some idea of what this difficulty is, think of the other arts for a moment. Is it possible to enjoy them without paying attention to them? More specifically, can you enjoy a painting without looking at it? Can you enjoy poetry without reading it? Can you enjoy a play without watching it?

Of course your answer to each of these questions has to be no. We may not like a painting but we have to look at it first before we can decide. And it is impossible to judge a poem without first reading it. In other words, to enjoy painting, drama, sculpture, literature, poetry, and dance, we have to at least look at them and pay attention to them. Otherwise, we won't even know that they're there!

But now ask yourself one more question: Is it possible to enjoy music without listening to it?

The Lost Art of Listening . . .

The answer is yes. We can indeed enjoy music without listening to it. We do just that every day of our lives. The radio plays while we study and we enjoy what we hear while concentrating on something else. We aren't listening. Or we watch a drama on television. In the background we hear a sound track, but our attention is on the drama. We hear the music but we don't listen. In an elevator, a tape plays while we ride up or down. But we are thinking of something else. The music is pleasant and we enjoy it, but we aren't really listening.

Unlike the other arts, music is all around us every day. We know it is there because it makes an impression on our ears. But most of us have gotten lazy. It's become too easy to allow music to make that initial impression but go no further. In other words, it frequently never reaches our brains.

If we are going to understand music, we're going to have to work at it. Understanding music requires an effort on the part of the listener. It is not enough to allow music to drift through the air, occasionally causing us to think, but most often giving us only a pleasant feeling and nothing else. Instead, we are going to have to concentrate.

Even with no knowledge of music theory, you will find that careful listening can tell you a lot about what the composer of the music had in mind. Try listening seriously to a few of your favorite popular songs. Concentrate! What are the lyrics saying? Do they mean anything or are they just nonsense? What do you enjoy most about each song? Which is more important in each—the melody or the rhythm?

Remember, composers don't write music solely for their own pleasure. They want to have some effect on you. They don't want their music to drift by your ears without you noticing it. They want you to listen. It takes practice, but the more you really listen, the more you will understand the music they have written.

. . . And Listening Again

Think back to the charts which followed the introduction to this book. There you saw listed many different types of music, some of which you may not be familiar with. But of those you know, can you honestly say that you *like* all of them? For example, do you like modern jazz? Do you enjoy Baroque classical music? Could you spend hours every day listening to traditional American folk songs?

Most of us are willing to admit that there are some kinds of music that we can live without. Although we recognize that many people enjoy such music, for some reason we find it boring. Just for an illustration, let's suppose that modern jazz affects you this way. A friend of yours is playing a record by trumpeter Miles Davis and you say to yourself, "That's just noise. It doesn't sound right. It's dull. I don't have any idea what is going on."

A common mistake made by many of us in such instances is to dismiss the music as a fraud. We try to convince ourselves that the people who buy records of such music are being tricked. They don't really like the music. They simply pretend to, in order to impress others.

Let's go back to our illustration. We said a number of things about the Miles Davis record, but the most revealing was the last: "I don't have any idea what is going on." This is the key to understanding why some people like Miles Davis and some don't. Those who like him probably have an understanding of what is happening in his records. Listeners who are ignorant of the ingredients of his music, its style, its form, and its history, cannot possibly be expected to like it.

Of course, it is possible to understand what is going on in a Miles Davis record and still not like it. In this case, an honest judgment has been made. The listener has tried. The result is a continued distaste for Davis's music. Instead of criticizing others who enjoy Davis, the open-minded listener simply recognizes that such music is not for him or her.

The honest judgment cannot be made, then, without an attempt to understand. And strangely, the way to make that attempt is to listen intently to music that you don't like! If you find Beethoven's music to be boring, make your final judgment concerning him only after you have listened to him for days or weeks or even months. After the passage of a few years, go back to him and try again.

Listen to Beethoven

Read about him. Study his ideas. Give him every chance to prove himself. In the end, you may find that you still don't like his music. But at least your final judgment will be based on knowledge, not ignorance.

Your approach should be the same for all other areas of music. Don't judge country music until you have listened to it again and again. Don't judge opera until you have listened to many operas.

The first key to understanding music is listening to it, intensely and repeatedly. Remember that every style of music has something to offer you. But if you fail to find it because you didn't give it a chance to be discovered, you have no one to blame but yourself.

STUDY ACTIVITIES

1. Look at the following list of kinds of music. Decide which of them you like and which you dislike. Then indicate your feeling by checking the appropriate space.

	Like	*Dislike*	*Not Sure*
a. Classical Music	______	______	______
b. Blues	______	______	______
c. Opera	______	______	______
d. Musical Comedy	______	______	______
e. Rock and Roll	______	______	______
f. Soul Music	______	______	______
g. Jazz	______	______	______
h. Country Music	______	______	______
i. Symphonies	______	______	______
j. Chamber Music	______	______	______

   Now go back and think about the kinds of music you said you disliked. Have you honestly given each of them a fair chance to prove itself?

2. Many parents complain that rock and roll music is nothing more than meaningless noise.
   a. Have they really listened?
   b. If so, why might they still feel as they do?
   c. If not, will dedicated listening cause them to begin to like rock and roll?

3. Suppose a teenaged boy has been kept isolated from music all of his life. When his fifteenth birthday arrives, he has never heard a note of music. Then, as a birthday present, one record of each of the styles listed in 1 (above) is played for him. Will he like the sounds of all the styles equally? Or will he prefer some styles over others?

4. Listen to a record by one of your favorite groups. Be sure to choose one in which the group plays by itself and not with an orchestral accompaniment. As you listen, try to answer each of the following questions:
   a. How many instruments are playing?
   b. How many people are singing?

c. Concentrate on the sound of two of the instruments. Which one is playing the higher notes?

d. Which do you like best about the record—the melody, the beat, or the lyrics? Or is there some other factor you find appealing?

e. Is it possible for you to concentrate on the sound of a *single* instrument so intently that you can no longer hear the rest of the music?

5. Some people like jazz and some people don't. Assuming that all have given jazz a decent opportunity to prove itself, why might this be?

6. A proverb of the Passamaquoddy Indians says, "Never judge a man until you have walked thirty days in his moccasins." What do you think the proverb has to say about what you have read in this chapter?

Chapter 2

MELODY

At first hearing, a piece of music often seems to be a rather complicated mass of sound. Instruments are playing. Perhaps someone is singing. The sound seems to change every second. If we're going to analyze what is going on, where in all of this should we start?

The Melody

The best answer is that we should start where the composer probably started—at the melody. The melody is simply the succession of notes which stands out above all the rest of the music. Sometimes we call it the "tune." If the composer wrote a strong melody, the whole piece, whether it be a song or an entire movement of a symphony, revolves around the melody. If the composer wrote a weak melody, it can still dictate the structure of the piece, but in a negative fashion. That is, the weakness of the melody forces some other element of the music into prominence. The melody itself becomes an item of secondary importance.

You might be wondering just what constitutes a strong melody and what constitutes a weak one. Of course, one answer might be that the strength of a melody is nothing more than a matter of opinion. What one person considers to be a beautiful succession of notes, rising and falling in just the right way, may to another person be dull and quickly forgotten.

Actually, the strength of a melody goes beyond this. The simple fact is that a few composers have been able to write melodies which nearly everyone finds to be beautiful and full of life. They are strong melodies. Some people may not like what the composer does with the melody. They may think the composer is mistaken in the way he or she ties it in with the rest of the composition. But the bare melody itself has undeniable strength.

As examples of this kind of melody, try listening to two themes, first one by the Austrian composer Franz Schubert, then one by Paul McCartney. With

Schubert, listen to the second principal melody in the first movement of his *Eighth Symphony*. You can hear the melody a little more than a minute after the beginning of the symphony, following a long note held by the French horns. The theme is played first by the cellos, then by the violins. With McCartney, try to get the Beatles' *Abbey Road* album and listen to "Golden Slumbers." As you listen to these melodies, try to eliminate all the other sounds of the pieces from your mind. Concentrate only on the melodies.

You are, of course, free to disagree with the statement that these two themes are strong melodies. All that can be said in support of the claim that they have strength is that most people who have heard these melodies have liked them and remembered them. They have found them pleasant to hum or sing to themselves.

Memorability, then, is one of the characteristics of a strong melody. A melody with this quality has the strength to dictate the course of the entire piece of music of which it is a part.

Some people would go further and state that a strong melody is also lyrical. That is, it has a smoothness or a softness which seems to give it a singing quality. Both the Schubert and the McCartney melodies are examples of lyricism. The notes follow one another in an even, predictable manner. They don't jump around abruptly.

Nevertheless, there are melodies of undeniable strength which *do* jump around. Listen to the opening theme of Beethoven's *Third Symphony*. The first eight notes of the theme are all distinctly separated from one another. There is no smooth flow from one note to the next. Still, the melody has a quality which makes it hard to forget. If you listen to the entire first movement of the symphony, you'll see that the opening theme has a power which shapes the course of the entire movement. It has strength. It is memorable: but it isn't lyrical.

Again, you are certainly free to disagree. Perhaps you feel that Beethoven's melody *is* lyrical. We could argue about this. But here's a challenge. After listening carefully to the whole movement, try to forget those eight notes of the opening melody. If after a few hours or a few days you haven't succeeded, you're merely witnessing the fact that it is memorable. Though the theme may or may not be lyrical, it is certainly difficult to forget. And in its memorability lies its strength.

What About Weak Melodies?

On the other hand, there are melodies which are not strong. You are not likely to want to whistle them. Two more examples will help to make this clear.

Listen first to the opening half-minute or so of Igor Stravinsky's *Rite of Spring*. Now, perhaps with a little practice you *could* sing the Stravinsky melody. But the question is: Do you want to? Probably not. It doesn't have the easy-to-remember quality we expect in a strong melody. It seems angular and unpredictable. More than anything, it's confusing.

But Stravinsky may have had another reason for choosing his melody. Perhaps he simply wanted to create a mood. Or maybe he wished to create an abstract pattern to prepare you mentally for the rest of the composition.

Listen next to the entire *Rite of Spring*. If you find the piece difficult, don't give up. Concentrate! Remember what you learned in the last chapter. Give Stravinsky every chance to prove himself.

When you have listened to the entire compositon, try to answer the following question: What reasons might Stravinsky have had for choosing the kind of melody he used at the opening of the *Rite of Spring*?

Another example of a weak melody can be found in the first song of the *Abbey Road* album—"Come Together," by John Lennon. Listen to the song a few times. Then hum or whistle the first 25 notes of the melody. You will find that there are just three different notes repeated over and over again. Certainly the melody can be remembered, but by itself it is still boring. What we really like about the song are the sensuous beat and the strange, irresistible lyrics. Feast your ears on those incredible word combinations—"monkey finger," "walrus gumboot," "spinal cracker." Lennon chose a weak melody which wouldn't interfere with his lyrics. The music stays in the background. Its purpose is to support the words of the song. They are important. And as a result, it is the words we remember. When we feel like singing "Come Together," we sing the words, not the melody.

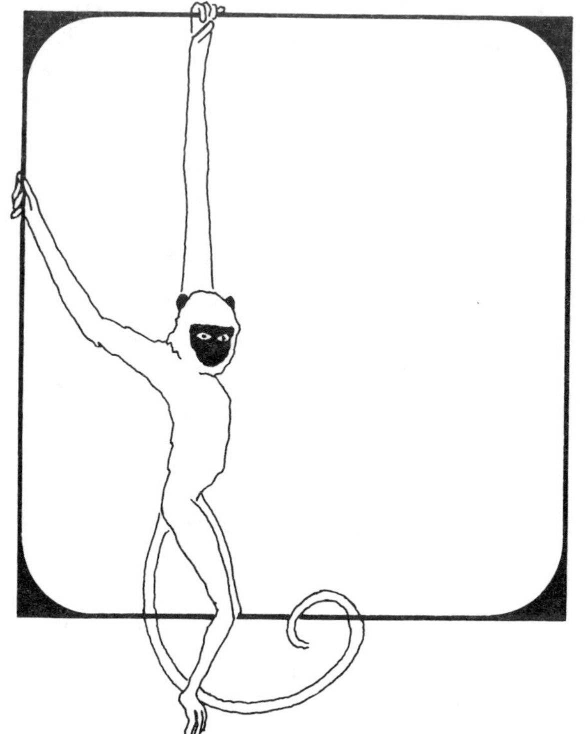

Which Kind Is Better?

But all of this is not to say that Schubert and McCartney wrote good melodies while Stravinsky and Lennon wrote bad ones. In melodic writing, "strong" and "weak" are *kinds* of melodies. They have nothing to do with quality. In other words, our judgment of whether a melody is good should not be based on whether we can remember it. Instead, we should consider the contribution made by the melody to the entire composition of which it is a part. If the melody serves a purpose, as both the Stravinsky and the Lennon melodies do, then calling it "bad" makes no sense.

Thus, in trying to understand a melody, we should consider the intentions of the composer. If we can see what the composer is trying to do, then we can gain some insight into the purpose of the melody.

Melody and History

It is no accident that the Stravinsky melody seemed a bit disjointed. A large percentage of the melodies of classical music which have been written in the twentieth century have just this quality. They are difficult to sing. In this respect, they are totally unlike the many beautiful and easy-to-remember melodies written during the Romantic period of the nineteenth century.

One of the reasons for this difference is the fact that many contemporary composers have consciously tried to move away from traditional sounds. They feel that the rules which governed composition during the nineteenth century were too restrictive. The music of that period was too predictable.

Thus, modern composers are investigating new tonal systems. They are trying completely new methods of composing music. Their wish is to create sounds totally outside our everyday experience.

Stravinsky was one of the first of the new composers. So we shouldn't be surprised that the melody in *Rite of Spring* seemed a bit strange. At first we viewed that melody only as it related to the composition in which it appeared. But now we should see that the melody has meaning from a larger, historical standpoint. It was an example of a *new* sound. Stravinsky didn't want it to be whistled, as nineteenth-century themes were. He wanted it to be disjointed, angular, and unpredictable. He was working in a particular historical framework, the framework of modern twentieth-century music. He created themes to reflect that framework.

So we see that the *Rite of Spring* melody served Stravinsky's purposes in a number of ways. It strengthened the composition itself. And it settled that composition into a specific historical framework.

Improvisation

There is a totally different kind of melody which has become of great importance in the twentieth century. That is the *improvised* melody. Improvised melodies are made up by performers spontaneously while they play. They don't think about these melodies beforehand or practice them. When the time comes to play, they place their confidence in their talent, skill, and inspiration—and begin playing!

In our terms, we might call improvised melodies weak because they are hard for an audience to remember. You wouldn't find yourself humming one of these melodies on the way to school. Yet in another respect, they are among the strongest melodies which can possibly be created, for they are generated in the mind of the performer and explode immediately into sound without ever being written down.

Improvisation has reached its greatest development in the area of music known as jazz. It is the backbone of jazz. In fact, one of the best definitions of jazz which can be given is that it is music that is at least partially improvised.

Recently, composers of classical music have seen the great potential offered by improvisation. Works are now being written for symphony orchestras in which members of the orchestra are allowed to play whatever they want at various places in the composition.

You may think that improvisation in music would lead to complete chaos. Not at all! An improvised melody isn't a free-for-all. It is similar to a written melody in that there are rules governing what can be played. Using their own judgments, the performers decide what rules are in effect. Their decisions tell them how limited they are in their freedom to express themselves.

An improvised melody, however, is unlike a written melody in that it is always changing. Good jazz musicians rarely repeat themselves. In a song or symphony we expect to hear the principal melody again and again. But in a jazz performance we become suspicious of a soloist's skill if we hear the same melody repeatedly.

Understanding an improvised melody requires a different approach from that we would use with a written melody. When we listen to a jazz soloist we should be aware of the fact that we are hearing both a composer writing music while we listen, and a performer playing and interpreting that music immediately and as skillfully as possible.

Listening to Jazz

When you listen to jazz, keep the following points in mind:

1. The melody played by the soloist is *not* supposed to sound like the melody of the original song on which it is based. Instead, the soloist tries to play

around that original melody, improving it, making it more interesting and reflective of his or her own personality.

2. The soloist is displaying performing skills as well as composing skills.

3. Instead of creating melodies that you will want to sing, the soloist wants to affect you emotionally, to play melodies that will make you think and feel.

4. Jazz is a deeply personal art form. More than anything, jazz soloists are expressing what is inside themselves. Although they hope to reach you with their music, they are also trying to reach themselves. What you hear are their deepest feelings, expressed musically the very moment they occur.

You can see that it is just as difficult to say what is good and what is bad with improvised melodies as it was with written melodies. You can criticize a jazz performer's skills or originality. But it's almost impossible to say that the soloist played a "bad" melody. Such a conclusion implies that you think that there is something wrong *inside* the performer.

Of course, you may simply not *like* a particular jazz performance. If you feel that you have listened carefully and that you have given the performer every chance to reach you, then you certainly have a right to draw this conclusion. You are saying only that the soloist failed to affect you with his or her choice of melodies.

To get a feeling for the sound of jazz, listen to at least two recorded performances. The "Listening List" makes a few recommendations concerning musicians you might enjoy hearing. Of course, there's no reason for you to stop your investigation of jazz after just two performances. Listen to jazz at every opportunity. When you do, keep in mind all that has been said about improvised melody. As the performers create, think of their melodies as feelings flowing from deep inside them.

At the end, try to decide how *you* have been affected.

STUDY ACTIVITIES

1. Think of three of your favorite songs. Would you say that the melodies of these songs are strong or weak? What other factors besides strength or weakness of melody make the songs memorable for you?

2. Suppose that you are a composer and are asked to compose melodies for each of the following situations. In one or two sentences each, describe the kinds of melodies you might compose.

   a. A jingle is needed to advertise a new soft drink.

   b. A song is needed to celebrate the victory of an army.

   c. A political candidate needs a campaign song.

   d. A rock group wants a theme song.

   e. A television producer wants a melody to use as a background for a documentary about auto racing.

   f. A bride and groom want a wedding march.

   g. A song is needed for the dedication of a new cathedral.

3. Sometimes it is difficult to decide whether we like a song because of its melody or because of its lyrics. Think back to the song "Golden Slumbers" by Paul McCartney. Is it possible that some quality of the lyrics tricked us into thinking that we were listening to a beautiful melody? If so, what was there about the lyrics which might have done this?

4. Once again, you are going to be a composer! Suppose that your lyricist has given you the following pairs of lines to be used in several different songs. Create a melody for each pair of lines. If you know how to write music, jot down the melody. Don't feel that you have to use the first melody which pops into your head. Instead, try two or three different melodies for each set. Then decide which of them is the strongest and most memorable.

   a. Watch each mornin' for the comin' of the sun glow,
      Wait at dawn for the dyin' of the night.

   b. It was just a week ago I discovered I was someone
      Who could write a song as well as anybody that I know.

   c. Casey, where are you going?
      Back to the home that you knew?

   d. Fireflies, yellow eyes, shining by the stream,
      Winter cold, a marigold, floating through my dream.

Chapter 3

RHYTHM

One-two-three-four
One-two-three-four
One-two-three-four
One-two-three-four

If you have ever done any marching, you recognize the steady counting from one to four as the sound of the basic pattern which keeps everyone marching together.

Left-right, left-right
Left-right, left-right

There's an evenness to the sound which everyone can easily recognize.

By adding words, we can make the pattern a little more interesting:

White-green-red-blue
March-on-one-two
Blue-red-green-white
This-feels-just-right.

The steady pulse we feel running through all of these patterns is called the *beat*. It's the beat which keeps a group of marchers, or a piece of music, on the move. Even when the music gets very complicated, we can feel the beat somewhere in the background. To keep track of it we often tap our feet.

One-two-three-four
One-two-three-four

Let's change the words of our verse just a little.

White-green-red-blue
Marching-on-one-and-two
Blue-red-green-white
Give it a-chance, it-feels just-right.

Obviously, something has changed in addition to the words. Not the beat, of course, for we can still feel it pounding away in the background. But at a few places in the verse we have two or even three syllables to fit into a single beat. In the last line, for example, the three syllables "give it a" must be spoken in the same period of time as the one-syllable word "blue" was in the previous line.

The verse is now more interesting to repeat than simply one-two-three-four. We have made it more interesting by changing just one thing: the *rhythm.*

Rhythm here refers to the duration of each syllable in the verse. The three syllables "give," "it," and "a" are each spoken in only one third of the time used to speak the one-syllable word "blue." The two syllables in "marching" are each spoken in one half of the same period of time.

As another example of how rhythm can change our marching verse around, look at the following, slightly more complicated, version. You may have to read it over a few times in order to feel the rhythm properly. While you practice it, listen for the beat, the unchanging one-two-three-four in the background.

White and-green can make an-armadillo-blue

Marching is an-exercise-count it two by-two and if a

Blue and-red automobile-changes into-white

Anyone here would-give it a chance to-feel just-right.

This is not the only possible rhythm for this set of words. Can you create another?

Rhythm in Music

Rhythm in music is no different from rhythm in a marching verse. It refers simply to the length of the individual notes of a melody.

To see how this works, sing to yourself the eight notes of a descending scale, do-ti-la-so-fa-mi-re-do. If you aren't sure how to do this, your teacher will help you out.

Your descending scale is a melody in which each of the eight notes lasts for the same length of time. Now sing the first line of the familiar Christmas carol, "Joy to the World":

"Joy to the world, the Lord has come . . . ."

You'll see that you have sung exactly the same notes that you used in your descending scale, but you have changed the rhythm. Some notes have become longer than others. The basic pattern of the rhythm might be a little clearer if you read it as a marching verse:

One two three four
One two three four
Joy to the world, the
Lord is come. . . .

You can see that the two words, "to the," are sung in the same amount of time used for the word "joy." And the word "come" at the end uses two beats all for itself.

Rhythm Gives Music Its Character

This example shows you that melody and rhythm are closely tied together. Any melody that you hear must have a rhythm, even if it is only the dull rhythm which we heard in the descending scale. Thus it is vital for composers to consider rhythm when they are choosing their melodies. A simple melody can be made exciting if it is attached to a sparkling, complicated rhythm. But its entire character can be changed by giving it an easier, more conventional rhythm. To illustrate this point, listen to Frederic Chopin's *Prelude in C Minor* for the piano. As you listen, try to block the melody out of your mind. Concentrate only on the rhythm.

You'll find that Chopin used a very simple rhythmic pattern throughout the prelude. As a marching verse, we might indicate that pattern as follows:

One-two-three and-four
One-two-three and-four

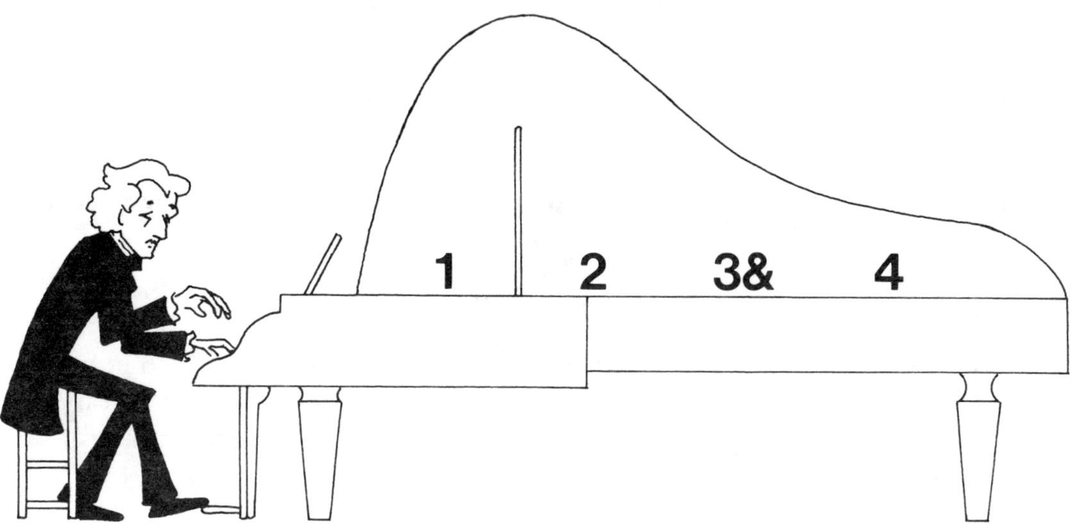

This simple rhythm characterizes the piece. And its simplicity gives the prelude a feeling which we wouldn't have sensed with a more complicated rhythm. The prelude seems calm, perhaps even reassuring. Or possibly you sensed that it was conveying sadness.

For contrast with the Chopin prelude, listen to an example of ragtime piano, a style that was popular at the beginning of the twentieth century. The "Listening List" at the beginning of this book names a few composers from whose works a good example of ragtime can be selected. As you listen to the piece, notice especially the complicated rhythmic patterns. Think of ways in which the ragtime composition contrasts with the Chopin prelude.

Composers of ragtime music purposely chose complicated rhythms for their songs. They realized that these rhythms gave their compositions an exciting quality which could rarely be matched in pieces using simpler rhythms. They tried to put accents in unexpected places. This gave the melody an uncertain quality, making it difficult to sense just what is going to happen next.

This trick of putting accents in unexpected places in a melody has been given a name. It's called *syncopation*. Syncopation was an important characteristic of early jazz, and it remains important even today in much of our modern music.

Listen once again to the ragtime composition. This time, see if you can spot the syncopation. Listen for unexpected accents in the melody. And at the same time, note how easy it is to pick out the steady beat of the piece, the heavy, unchanging one-two-three-four, one-two-three-four, which is always swinging along in the background.

From these two examples you can see how rhythm gives a melody its character. The type of rhythm which a composer uses gives the composition the desired feeling, regardless of the melody that was chosen.

Meter

All of the rhythms we have investigated so far have been built over our now familiar one-two-three-four, one-two-three-four. When a piece of music has this kind of a beat supporting it, it is said to be in *duple meter*. This means simply that the composition is divided into small groups of two or four beats. These are the beats we sense when we tap our feet two or four times during each phrase of the melody.

It's fair to say that nearly all Western music is written in duple meter. Whether it be classical, jazz, soul, country, or rock, one usually finds that the beats come in small groups of two or four.

But a small percentage of the total of all music is written in other meters. The most common of these other types is the *triple meter* composition.

To get a feeling for the triple meter, read the following verse to yourself:

High near the top of the maple tree
Waiting for sunlight to find her there
Soft in her nest sat the meadowlark.

Now pretend that you are going to march to this rather unmilitary poem. Let's divide it into beats:

High near the-top of the-maple tree
Waiting for-sunlight to-find her there
Soft in her-nest sat the-meadowlark.

In numbers we would write this poem:

One two three-one two three-one two three
One two three-one two three-one two three
One two three-one two three-one two three

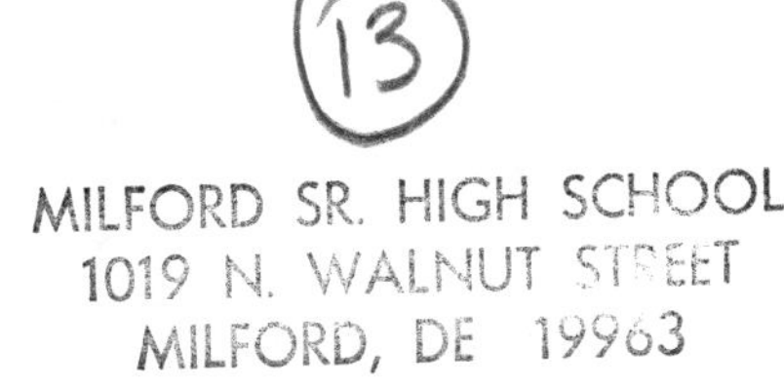

As you can easily see, there's nothing one-two-three-four about this poem. Its basic subdivisions are groups of three syllables each. The poem is in triple meter.

We can now extend the idea of triple meter to music. Compositions written in triple meter are based on small groups of three beats each. If you tap your foot to them, you'll tap in threes, rather than twos or fours.

As an example of a piece of music written in triple meter, listen to a waltz written by Johann Strauss. Remember that there are going to be rhythmic patterns which stand out over the basic beat. Try to eliminate these from your mind. Listen only for the one-two-three, one-two-three.

The waltz is a dance which came into prominence around 1800 and is still with us today, though without the popularity it once enjoyed. The chief characteristic of the waltz is that it is written in triple meter.

Unusual Meters

During the twentieth century, the use of meters other than duple or triple has become more common in both jazz and classical music. Though your understanding of music is not dependent on your developing a complete grasp of these rather complicated meters, you might enjoy listening to one. An excellent example is a composition written by Paul Desmond called "Take Five." As the title indicates, the basic subdivisions of the piece are small groups of five beats each. This is called *quintuple meter*. While you listen to the piece, try to hear the one-two-three-four-five, one-two-three-four-five—the driving force behind the composition.

Don't become confused by the rhythms which stand out above the basic beat of the piece. Listen for the pulse. Then, when you have found it, relax a little and enjoy the melodies improvised by first Paul Desmond, the saxophonist, and later by Dave Brubeck, the pianist.

"Take Five" ends with drummer Joe Morello improvising some very complicated rhythms over the quintuple meter. See if you can keep track of the five-beat pulse while he plays. But if you can't, don't despair. It takes a great deal of practice to follow quintuple meter. Our ears are used to twos and threes and fours, but not fives. Five seems a bit unnatural to us. It's no wonder that Western music got along perfectly well for thousands of years without even considering quintuple meter.

So in Summary . . .

Let's now look back over all of the ideas we have considered in this chapter. Melody, we saw, is nothing without rhythm. A composer chooses a rhythm which suits the melody and which helps to create the desired mood. The rhythms may be simple or they may be complex. But even the most complicated of them are built over a steady, unchanging pulse. The pulse is usually made up of small groups of two or four beats each. But occasionally a composition may consist of groups of three beats. And once in a while we'll run into a piece with groups of five or seven or even thirteen beats each.

To see how imaginatively rhythm can be handled by a skillful composer, listen to *El Salón México,* one of the most rhythmic pieces of music that has ever been composed. It was written by the contemporary American composer, Aaron Copland. Copland uses a relatively recent innovation in *El Salón México.* Rather than writing the entire piece in duple or triple or any other meter, he uses *all* of them! Thus, sometimes there will be a group of three beats followed by a group of seven beats, and this followed by a group of four beats. And the rhythms played over these beats are just as complicated.

Needless to say, *El Salón México* is a complex piece of music. You probably won't be able to follow it exactly, but you should find it very easy to enjoy. Listen to it as carefully as you can. At times listen only to the melody. At others, try finding the beat by tapping your foot. At still others, concentrate on the fantastic rhythms rushing along above the beat.

In the end, although you may not have been able to keep track of each and every beat, you probably will have gained some insight into what Copland tried to do in this piece. By combining bright and fresh melodies with driving, irresistible rhythms, he has created excitement. It's almost impossible not to be caught up in the happiness of *El Salón México.*

Understanding the piece, then, means not that we should understand each and every one of its details. It means only that we should understand the composer's intentions and the system he used to carry them out. Whether we like the piece remains a personal matter. But one thing is certain: we have made ourselves richer by listening.

STUDY ACTIVITIES

1. You have seen that every melody must have a rhythm associated with it. Is it possible to have a rhythm with no melody?

2. Decide which of the following lines from the Study Activities in Chapter 2 would best be set to music in duple meter and which would best be set in triple meter. You might decide that some would be satisfactory in either duple or triple meter:

   a. Watch each morning' for the comin' of the sun glow,
   Wait at dawn for the dyin' of the night.

   b. It was just a week ago I discovered I was someone
   Who could write a song as well as anybody that I know.

   c. Casey, where are you going?
   Back to the home that you knew?

   d. Fireflies, yellow eyes, shining by the stream,
   Winter cold, a marigold, floating through my dream.

3. Listen again to three of the compositions you studied in Chapter 2—*Rite of Spring*, "Golden Slumbers," and "Come Together." Then answer each of the following questions:

   a. How much emphasis does each composition place on rhythm?

   b. Which of the three compositions is most dependent on rhythm for its total effect?

   c. Which of the three compositions is least dependent on rhythm for its total effect?

4. A composer often must choose a rhythm which helps to express a particular emotion. You can test your own inventiveness at creating such rhythms. By tapping a pencil or clapping your hands, try to work out a rhythm which describes each of the following emotions. Feel completely free to express yourself. There are no right or wrong answers.

   a. Joy

   b. Nervousness

   c. Sadness

   d. Disgust

   e. Love

5. Suppose that you listened to "Take Five" but didn't realize that it was written in quintuple meter. Would you have enjoyed the piece *less* because you didn't realize this? Does knowledge of the special metrical characteristics of a piece of music help a listener to enjoy the music more?

6. How important are each of the following in causing a listener to enjoy a piece of music?

	Always	*Usually*	*Sometimes*	*Never*
a. The performers are talented.	______	______	______	______
b. The composer is famous.	______	______	______	______
c. The melody is beautiful.	______	______	______	______
d. The record has no scratches.	______	______	______	______
e. The lyrics describe an experience familiar to the listener.	______	______	______	______
f. The beat is easy to follow.	______	______	______	______
g. The rhythms are syncopated.	______	______	______	______
h. The rhythms are exciting.	______	______	______	______
i. The rhythms are complicated.	______	______	______	______
j. The rhythms are boring.	______	______	______	______

Chapter 4

HARMONY

Melody.

And rhythm.

Put them together and we can write any kind of music that we choose. They are the building blocks. They are the basis on which all music rests.

But perhaps you want to object just a bit. "O.K.," you say, "they are the building blocks. But when *I* listen to a piece of music, I hear a lot more than just a melody and some rhythm. Things still sound pretty complicated to me. In fact, I'd have to say that I hear lots of melodies, and they all seem to be mixed together."

If you have actually had some thoughts along these lines, congratulate youself, for you have come up with something positively brilliant. The great mass of sound which we hear in a symphony or in a popular song is nothing more than a large number of instruments playing melodies. Each instrument has its own melody. Played together, they produce the sound which we interpret as a musical composition.

Let's take a look at the ways in which two or more melodies can interact with each other. We'll be investigating an area of music theory which is known as *harmony*.

Harmony

Melodies, you will recall, are made up of individual notes. Suppose now that in a particular composition there are four melodies being played by four different instruments. Suppose further that we could stop the music and listen to what was happening at one single moment—one fraction of a second—in the piece. Think of what we would hear. Would it be four distinct melodies? Not at all! Instead, we would hear four single notes, one being played by each instrument.

Melodies interacting with each other, then, are really just individual notes interacting with each other. At any given moment in a composition we can stop the music and hear single notes sounding together. If there are three or more different notes being played, the resulting sound is called a *chord*. Harmony is the study of chords.

The most common of all chords is called the *triad*. To get an idea of what a triad sounds like, sing the second, third, and fourth words of the *Star-Spangled Banner*: "Oh, *say can you . . .* " Of course, to be a chord, the three notes of your triad must be sung simultaneously. Perhaps you can do this with two of your friends. Let one person sing the low note, "say," one person the middle note, "can," and the third person the high note, "you":

"you
can
say"

You'll find that the triad has a very pleasing sound. This quality, together with its simplicity, has caused it to be the most useful of all chords.

Many pieces of music consist almost entirely of simple triads. For example, nearly all country music has this characteristic. The same goes for the area of music known as the blues. An authentic blues, in fact, has a harmonic background based on a pattern of just three triads, repeated over and over again.

Other music is often made up of more complicated chords than the triad. But close analysis shows that nearly all of these chords can actually be constructed by performing one of the following operations on a simple triad:

1. Changing one or two of its notes slightly;
2. adding one or two notes to it, or
3. combining these two operations.

Consonance and Dissonance

We noticed that the triad seemed to have a pleasant sound. A chord with this quality is said to be *consonant*. Usually the question of what is consonant and what isn't is a matter of opinion. What some people regard as a pleasant sound is interpreted by others to be most disagreeable.

For example, a large percentage of modern classical music and jazz consists of harmonies based on chords which, at first hearing, don't sound consonant to many people. As a result, these people find the music difficult to enjoy. Chords which produce this result are called *dissonances*.

Dissonances seem to be in abundance today because many modern composers have become tired of using the same old triads. And in their search for new sounds, they have come up with some unusual chords which many listeners have found disagreeable. If you'll think back to the first chapter, you'll realize that the problem here is with the listeners, not the composers. Listeners must devote themselves to new sounds. They must listen to these compositions for hours, for days, for weeks, before making their judgments. And in the end, they'll probably realize that the difficulty with dissonance is no difficulty at all. Dissonance becomes consonance in the ears of the experienced listener, who realizes that the composer with a reason for using new and unusual chords should by all means use them.

You can get a better idea of how dissonance gradually comes to be accepted as consonance by listening to the works of Richard Wagner and Claude Debussy. Try the prelude to Wagner's opera, *Tristan und Isolde*. Follow this with Debussy's piano composition, *La Cathédrale Engloutie*. You may be surprised to find out that the sounds of both of these works were once thought by many people to be extremely unpleasant. Critics were shocked, and said that both works were filled with dissonant chords. But *Tristan* was written more than 100 years ago, and the Debussy composition, more than 50. In the intervening period of time, standards have changed. Now when we listen, we find that the chords of both pieces are quite agreeable. Today we judge them to be consonant.

Now listen to a modern classical composition. Try a work by Elliott Carter, David Diamond, Henry Cowell or Wallingford Riegger. At first you might feel as the first listeners to *Tristan und Isolde* felt. But don't jump to conclusions. Give the music a chance to become a part of you. Today the chords might seem dissonant. But in time, they may well become as consonant to you as the sound of the simplest triad.

Vertical Harmony

When we first considered the triad, we saw that the notes of the chord could be thought of as being built one on top of the other. To make this clearer, we diagrammed the three words of the *Star-Spangled Banner* vertically:

"you
can
say"

Some music consists of single chords much like our triad, following each other one by one, but distinctly separated from one another. We could diagram this type of music as follows:

notes of chord 1	notes of chord 2	notes of chord 3	notes of chord 4
A	D	G	J
B	E	H	K
C	F	I	L

Such music is said to consist of *vertical harmonies*. The characteristic sound which results arises from the vertical stacking of notes. The individual notes of each chord are dependent on the other notes of the chord to help give the music its special quality.

You can hear a beautiful example of vertical harmony at the beginning of the second movement of Dvořák's *New World Symphony*. Listen carefully and you'll be able to pick out seven distinct chords. Notice how each chord consists of stacks of notes. Each single note by itself would be dull. But by interacting with each other, the notes produce a lush, full sound.

Vertical harmony forms the basis for much of our folk music and many of our church hymns. And one of the richest sounds that has ever been invented, a sound which goes by the strange name of "barbershop harmony," is completely dependent on it. A fine example of barbershop harmony can be found in the song, "Lida Rose," from Meredith Willson's musical comedy, *The Music Man*.

"Lida Rose" illustrates a point that was made at the beginning of this chapter. At first hearing, the song sounds complex. But when we analyze it, we see that it consists of four separate melodies. Each performer sings one of the melodies. The individual notes of the melodies interact with each other and form single chords. These chords are nothing more than vertical stackings of notes. One chord follows another with neat precision—and the result is the lovely song, "Lida Rose."

Horizontal Harmony

With vertical harmony, we found that individual notes were dependent on the other notes which lay above them or below them in the chord. This vertical dependence produced the effect of single chords marching along, one after the other.

A second important type of harmony occurs when the notes of each melody are dependent on other notes which come *before* them or follow *after* them in the same melody. In this case, melodies are more or less *independent* of other melodies which lie above or below them. We call the harmonies which result from such independent melodies *horizontal* harmonies.

The word "harmony" here still refers to chords which consist of notes from different melodies sounding at the same time. Horizontal harmony, then, unquestionably has a vertical quality. But this vertical character is minor. We don't sense the effect of single chords following one another. Instead, we are more aware of the importance of individual melodies. Each one seems to have a character of its own. Occasionally we will hear the individual notes of the melodies sounding all at once, thus stacking themselves vertically, but these instances seem almost to be accidents. They allow us to orient ourselves momentarily, perhaps to identify a chord, but then the melodies are off and running on their individual paths again.

The following diagram might make the idea of horizontal harmony a little clearer to you. Suppose that one melody consists of single notes labeled with the letters A through G. A second melody is labeled H through N. And a final melody is labeled O through U. These three melodies form a section of a piece of music. By careful listening, we are able to take this section apart and diagram it as follows:

Melody 1:	A	B		C				D	E	F		G
Melody 2:		H	I	J	K	L			M		N	
Melody 3:	O		P	Q		R	S		T			U

You can see that at only two places have the individual notes stacked themselves vertically to form a chord. The rest of the time they sound only by themselves, or perhaps with one other note. The melodies are really quite independent of each other. They are important in their own right, not just in how they relate to the other melodies.

Of course, a composer using horizontal harmonies must be careful to choose melodies which are not *totally* independent. Otherwise the listeners will most certainly become confused. They might think that they are listening to three or four different compositions at once! Thus, the skillful composer chooses melodies which have a certain amount of independence, but which interact with each other vertically just enough so we can keep our bearings.

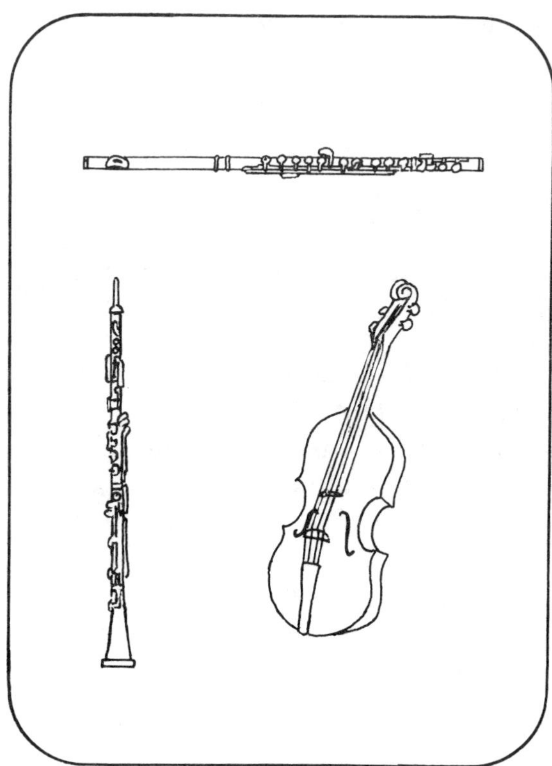

Johann Sebastian Bach was one of the most skillful composers who ever lived. His genius in the composing of works based on horizontal harmonies reflects this fact. Listen to the middle movement of his *Brandenburg Concerto No. 2.* Here a flute, an oboe, and a violin are each given wonderful melodies, each with its own character and charm. We have no difficulty thinking of them as independent melodies. But at the same time, we marvel at how they fit together, weaving their ways around and about each other and giving us just enough of a sense of vertical harmony that we don't become lost.

Other examples of such music can be found in the string quartets of Beethoven and Brahms. And more recent examples are provided by some of the big-band compositions of Duke Ellington. Ellington often gives one melody to his saxophone section, another to his trombones, and a third to his trumpets. These melodies retain their independence while threading themselves together in the same incredible manner that Bach's melodies displayed in his *Brandenburg Concerto*.

Combining Horizontal with Vertical

Much of our popular music, soul music, and country music displays combinations of horizontal and vertical harmonies. The singer or singers normally sing a melody of such importance that it has horizontal independence. But backing up the singer are usually three or four dependent melodies which are stacked vertically in simple chords, many of them triads.

And most longer works for orchestra, you'll soon discover, consist of individual sections, some of them consisting of mostly vertical harmonies and some of them, horizontal. As usual, careful and persistent listening will tell you which is which.

A Few Recommendations

As you listen to music, especially complicated music, you should try to discover how the melodies are interacting with each other. Try to pick out the individual melodies played by each instrument. Hunt for obscure melodies, far in the background. Then ask yourself these questions: Are the melodies independent, coming together only occasionally to allow us to get our bearings? Or are they dependent on each other, stacking themselves into individual chords which follow one another in an easily discernible pattern?

Don't worry about not being able to name individual chords. Instead, look for broad relationships among melodies. If you can see how individual melodies affect each other harmonically, you will have come a long way toward understanding what is happening inside a piece of music.

STUDY ACTIVITIES

1. The diagram on page 29 showed how three melodies could interact horizontally. Using a similar diagram, show how the same melodies would appear if they were interacting vertically. Represent melody 1 by the letters A though G, melody 2 by the letters H through N, and melody 3 by the letters O through U.

2. Decide which of the following are examples of vertical harmony and which are examples of horizontal harmony:

	Vertical	*Horizontal*
The Chopin *Prelude in C Minor* (You may wish to listen to the prelude again before deciding.)	______	______
Three people singing the "round," *Three Blind Mice*	______	______
A crowd at a baseball game singing *The Star-Spangled Banner*	______	______
An orchestra holding the final note of a symphony	______	______
A robin and a sparrow singing	______	______
People at a party singing "For He's a Jolly Good Fellow"	______	______
A jazz trumpeter and a jazz trombonist improvising melodies simultaneously	______	______

3. A difficult assignment: Give as many possible explanations as you can for the fact that certain chords sound dissonant to some people while those same chords sound consonant to other people.

4. Listen to two songs by a small group which you especially enjoy. Then answer the following questions:
   a. Is there anything in either of these songs that your parents would label "dissonant"?
   b. How many instruments are playing in each song?
   c. How many singers are there in each song?
   d. Listen carefully to the melodies played by each instrumentalist. Would you characterize these melodies as dependent or independent?

Chapter 5

Acoustics

Acoustics is the science of sound. Perhaps you've never thought of the investigation of sounds as a science. But, in fact, sound has properties which can easily be studied in the laboratory. This chapter will focus on some of the more important findings of acoustic scientists. Much of what has been learned can be used to gain a better understanding of the inner workings of music.

Producing Sounds

You are probably familiar with the fact that the sound of your voice is produced by the vibration of your vocal chords. The chords are elastic membranes which are easily set in motion when air is forced between them. This method of producing sound illustrates the principle utilized by all musical instruments. First, there must be some sort of an elastic body present in the instrument. And second, this body must be caused to vibrate to produce a sound.

In stringed instruments, such as the violin and the guitar, the strings themselves are the elastic bodies. By plucking or bowing them, the performer causes them to vibrate. Brass and woodwind instruments are quite different. They all contain an enclosed column of air as their elastic body.

By vibrating the lips against a mouthpiece (with brass instruments), or by vibrating a small reed in the mouthpiece (with woodwinds), the performer causes the enclosed column of air itself to vibrate. A percussion instrument (for example, a drum, xylophone, or cymbal) produces sound when its sounding agent, either a stretched membrane (as in a drum) or a solid material (as in a xylophone) is struck, shaken, or otherwise made to vibrate.

Stringed, brass, woodwind, and percussion instruments have been with us for centuries. During the past few decades, electronic instruments, an entirely new class of instruments, have come into prominence. Although they can be extraordinarily complex, their method of producing sound is no different from that of a violin or a trumpet: they must cause an elastic body to vibrate. The first useful electronic instrument, the theremin, invented in 1920, produced sound by causing high frequency circuits to vibrate. Today's mainstays, the voltage-controlled synthesizer and the digital synthesizer, process electrical signals internally, using filters and oscillators. The electrical signals themselves remain silent: they produce sound, or music, only when they cause the diaphragm in a loudspeaker to vibrate.

Vibration, then, is the key to the production of sound. Understanding this one fact can help you understand even so complicated a process as the production of sound from a phonograph record. Suppose an orchestra is performing in a recording studio. First, the elastic bodies in the instruments of the orchestra vibrate. This etches an electronic vibration pattern into a tape. The tape is later played back in the studio, causing a needle to vibrate and cut a wavy pattern into a master recording disc. The disc presses this same pattern into the record which you buy and play on your turntable. The wavy pattern cut into your record makes your phonograph needle vibrate. This vibration is transformed into an electronic impulse which causes your loudspeaker to vibrate. The air between the loudspeaker and your ears now begins to vibrate. And finally—finally!—the air causes your eardrums to vibrate. Result: you hear the sound of the orchestra in the recording studio.

If the playback vehicle is a tape recorder, the vibration pattern produced by the orchestra is transferred to the cassette tape which you snap into your cassette machine. If it is a compact disc player, the pattern is cut into the disc in pits of varying depths by a laser. When the disc is played back, another laser beam scans the pits and is reflected and scattered by them. The beam is read by an optical sensor which converts the varying intensities of light into digital signals. These, in turn, are converted into impulses which cause a loudspeaker diaphragm to vibrate, thereby producing sound.

Sound Is Transmitted by Waves

All of these vibrations have certain basic characteristics that can easily be studied in the laboratory. The vibrations move back and forth in the direction in which the sound is traveling, producing a sound "wave." If you could see a moving sound wave, it would appear something like this.

Notice how the wave moves in "pulses" caused by condensations of molecules in the air (or whatever medium the wave is traveling through). Between pulses the molecules spread out. The distance between pulses is called a *cycle*. On the wave above, you can see three complete cycles.

Of course, sound waves can't all look alike. If they did, all music would sound the same. We wouldn't be able to distinguish the different notes of a melody. We wouldn't hear the high and low notes of vertical harmonies.

Waves can differ in two ways.

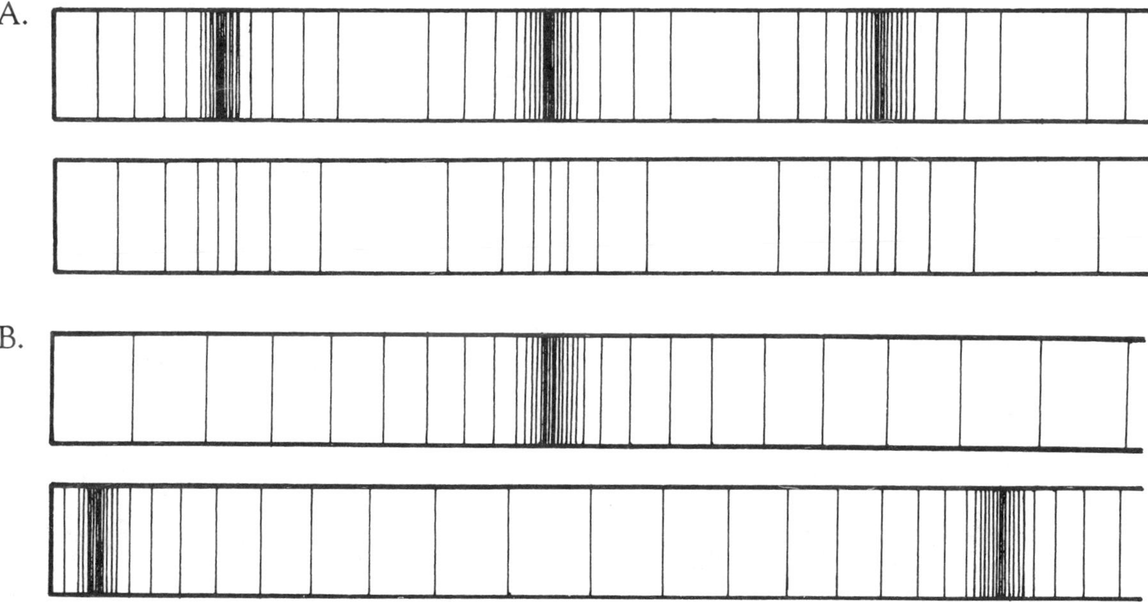

In example A, you can see that the individual cycles on the top wave are tighter or denser than the corresponding cycles on the bottom wave. These two waves are said to differ in *amplitude.* Amplitude is a measure of the intensity of a wave.

In example B, the waves have the same density, so there is no difference in amplitude. There are, however, more complete cycles in the same amount of space on the bottom wave than there are on the top wave. The bottom wave has two cycles; the top, only one. Thus, in a given time interval, you would hear two times as many cycles from the bottom wave as you would from the top. The number of complete cycles you hear every second is called the *frequency* of the wave. In example B, then, the two waves differ in frequency.

So far, this may all seem a bit abstract. Perhaps you're wondering just what this has to do with what you actually *hear* when a melody is played by a musical instrument. To find out, let's take a practical example. Suppose we pluck a string on a guitar. We know that the string will vibrate, setting up a wave that causes the air to vibrate, which, in turn, causes our eardrums to vibrate. Simply speaking, the *louder* the sound, the greater the amplitude of the wave. And the *higher* the note which is sounded, the greater the frequency.

The following laws sum up the relationship between sound and waves:

1. Amplitude affects the loudness or softness of a sound.
2. Frequency affects the highness or lowness of a sound.

Going back to our example of *The Star-Spangled Banner* from the last chapter, you can now see that the second, third, fourth, and fifth words are sung to notes which differ in frequency:

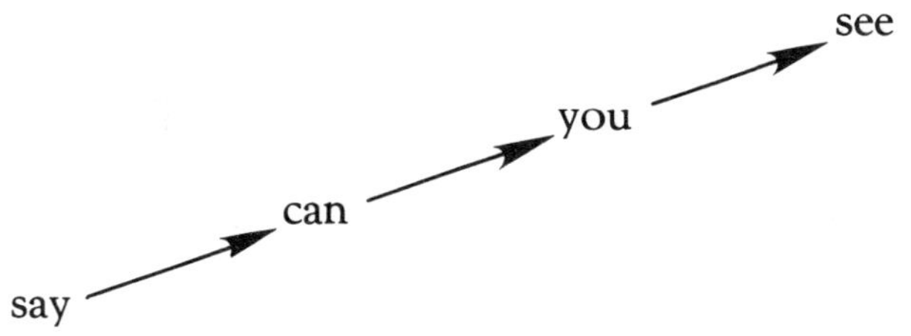

Each succeeding word is sung to a higher note. The frequency of the wave increases with each word. There are more complete cycles being produced every second. And if you choose to sing each word louder than the previous word, the amplitude will also increase.

The Limits of Our Hearing

A few specific numbers will give you a better feeling for the idea of frequency. If you press the bottom key on a piano, the one farthest to the left, you'll hear the lowest note that a piano is capable of producing. It is caused by a string vibrating 27½ times every second. We say that the note has a frequency of 27½ cycles per second.

As you are now well aware, the air also vibrates 27½ times per second when you press that key on the piano. And so does your eardrum. But that frequency is nearly as slow as your eardrum is capable of vibrating while still allowing you to sense its movement. A slightly lower frequency of around 16 cycles per second is the lowest sound that a person of normal hearing ability can perceive.

On the other hand, the highest note produced by a piano has a frequency of around 4,000 cycles per second. You are quite capable of hearing sounds much higher, up to about 20,000 cycles per second. But beyond this upper limit, your eardrums are not sensitive enough to perceive sounds.

Overtones

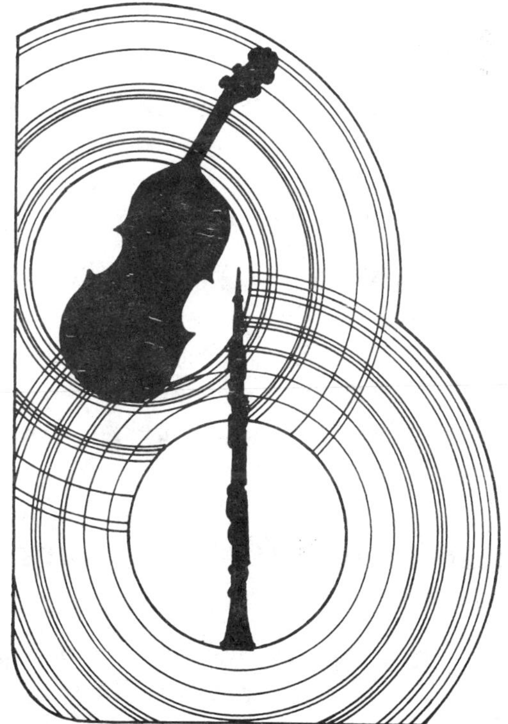

Amplitude and frequency are two of the characteristics which distinguish a sound wave. But together they are still not quite enough to completely characterize a wave. To see why this is so, imagine a melody being played first by a violin and then by an oboe. The two melodies are exactly the same, so the frequencies which reach our ears are the same. And if the violin and oboe play at the same volume, the amplitudes of the two waves are the same also. Seemingly, there is no difference between the two waves. Yet there *must* be, for our ears hear a violin first, then an oboe. In other words, although there is no difference in the amplitudes and frequencies which we perceive, we still have no difficulty whatsoever in sensing that the first melody and the second are somehow different. One melody has a quality about it that we recognize as being produced by a violin. The second melody has the quality of an oboe.

To understand what causes this difference in the quality of two sounds, it is necessary to return for a moment to our discussion of frequency. Let's concentrate our attention on a note which has a frequency of 100 cycles per second. If this note is being produced by a violin string, we know that the string is vibrating 100 times every second. But closer investigation reveals that *part* of the violin string is vibrating at 200 cycles per second; part is vibrating at 300 cycles per second; in fact, small parts are vibrating at every frequency which is an exact multiple of 100 cycles per second. The frequency which the ear hears and identifies is the lowest of these, 100 cycles per second. This is called the *fundamental.* The higher frequencies we are only dimly aware of. They are called *overtones.*

Thus, when a *single* instrument plays a *single* note, a rather complicated array of frequencies results:

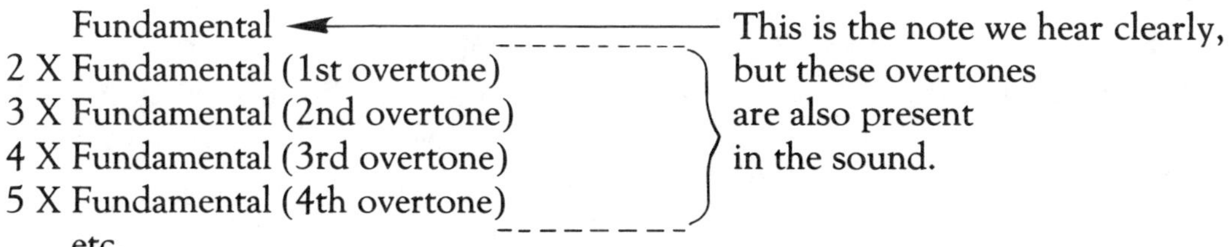

Now we're getting closer to the reason that the sound of a violin has a different quality about it than the sound of an oboe. Every instrument *favors* certain overtones. The violin, for example, favors the first overtone most strongly, and the third overtone about half as much. The second, fourth, fifth, and sixth overtones are hardly present at all in the sound of a violin. The oboe, on the other hand, favors the fourth and fifth overtones most strongly, and the sixth overtone only slightly less so. But the sound of the first three overtones is almost nonexistent. In other words, it is the *amplitude* of the various overtones that gives the sound of an instrument its particular quality.

Keep in mind that it is still the fundamental which we hear clearly. When two instruments play the same note, we hear the fundamental and realize that the two notes are identical. But almost subconsciously we also hear overtones. And since different instruments emphasize overtones, we are able to distinguish between two notes which are based on the same fundamental.

A Musical Color Chart

Music has borrowed a word from art to describe the quality of the sound produced by an instrument. The word is *color*, or sometimes, *tone color*. We say that the tone color of a trumpet is different from that of a guitar. This means that if a trumpet and a guitar play the same note at the same volume, we can still distinguish between the two sounds. As you have seen, we can do this because of overtones.

The word *timbre* means the same thing as tone color, and is often used as a synonym for it.

The chart on page 41 will give you a more accurate idea of the ability of various instruments to produce overtones. We might call it a "color chart." The chart assumes that each instrument is playing a note with a frequency of 100 cycles per second. The intensities (amplitudes) of the various overtones are indicated by the heights of the vertical bars.

Finally, Let's Listen to the Colors

The English composer Benjamin Britten has written a wonderful piece of music which enables us to hear separately the colors of all of the instruments of the orchestra. The composition is entitled *The Young Person's Guide to the Orchestra.* In it, you'll hear a melody, and variations of that melody, played individually by each of the following instruments: flutes and piccolo; oboes; clarinets; bassoons; violins; violas; cellos; double basses; harp; French horns; trumpets; trombones; and finally, percussion. Listen carefully to the composition and see how many of the instruments you can identify. Try to spot changes in color as the melody is passed from one set of instruments to the next. Think of the music as a wave of vibrations, passing from the phonograph, through the speaker and the air, and finally arriving at your ears. Listen for changes in the amplitude of the wave. And when the melody goes up or down, think of the wave as increasing or decreasing in frequency.

Britten

So What Are We—Scientists or Music Lovers?

Don't worry—we're still music lovers. The purpose of this chapter hasn't been to train you to think scientifically. Few experienced listeners ever consciously picture a wave passing from their phonographs to their ears. So after you have listened to the Britten composition once in this manner, you may never feel like doing it again. But it's important for you to realize the actual means by which sound is produced and transmitted to you. And it's enlightening to recognize just what it is about a wave that gives it loudness and softness, highness and lowness, and color. These facts you can hold in the back of your mind as you listen to music. And resting there, they can give you a fuller understanding of what music is all about.

Instrumental Colors: The Strength of Overtones

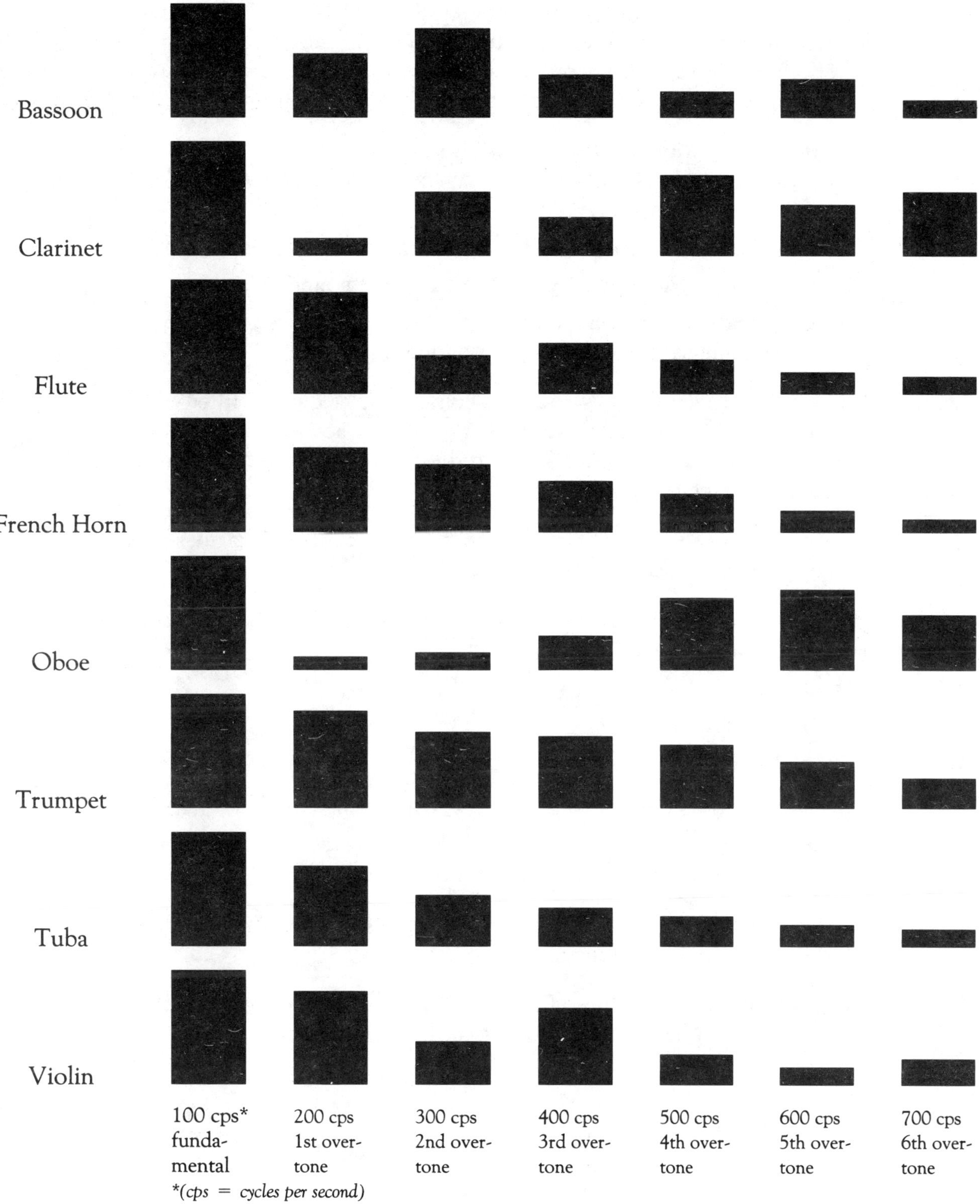

STUDY ACTIVITIES

1. Just as it is easy to distinguish between the sounds of two different instruments, so it is easy to distinguish between the sounds of two different speaking voices. What acoustic factors might cause one voice to sound different from a second voice?

2. In music, the word "pure" means "no overtones." In general, the fewer overtones a sound has, the purer that sound is considered to be. Referring to the chart on page 41,
   a. which instruments would you say produce the purest sounds?
   b. which instruments produce the least pure sounds?
   c. considering only the frequencies below 400 cycles per second, which instrument produces the purest sound?

3. Good stereo amplifiers sometimes come equipped with a filter which can eliminate all the sound waves with a frequency above 7,000 cycles per second if the listener desires. Often the filter is used when old or damaged records are being played. Why?

4. A guitar has six strings, each the same length. Yet the six strings produce six different notes. How is this possible?

5. Describe in as much detail as you can how sound is produced by each of the following musical instruments:
   a. Piano
   b. Harmonica
   c. Xylophone
   d. Organ
   e. Harp
   f. A blade of grass held between the fingers

6. A clarinet plays a note whose frequency is 440 cycles per second. What is the frequency of the fourth overtone?

7. A tuba plays a note whose fifth overtone has a frequency of 1,728 cycles per second. What is the frequency of the fundamental?

Chapter 6

FORM

Consider for a moment a piece of music that you especially enjoy. It might be a popular song, a symphony, or a jazz composition. If you stop to think just what it is about the music that you like, you'll probably find that it is the melody, the rhythm, the harmony, or some combination of these three. (If the composition is a song, there is of course a fourth possibility, the lyrics. But right now, we are considering just the music, not the words.) From what you have learned so far, this shouldn't be too surprising. After all, melody, rhythm, and harmony are the building blocks for all music. Compared to entire compositions, these three are short, easy to grasp, and easy to enjoy.

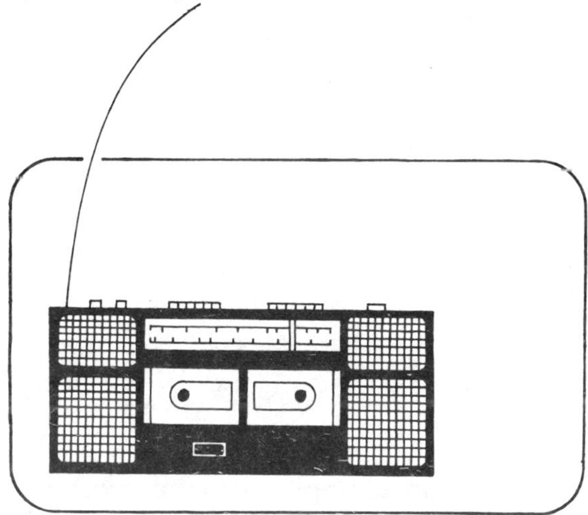

But when a large piece of music is put together, things become a bit more complicated. Whole sections aren't as easy to grasp as melodies or rhythms. So, if we don't wish to lose our way, we're going to ask just one small favor of the composer: every once in a while, if you don't mind, repeat those small phrases that we like. Repeat that melody which we found so appealing. Let us hear that interesting rhythm again. And now and then, weave your melodies together in the same way that you did earlier, so we don't lose sight of our favorite harmonies.

Thus, if you'll think back to that piece of music which you enjoy, you'll see that you really demand more than just nice melodies, rhythms, or harmonies. You demand further that they be repeated again and again. It's disappointing to hear a short section of music that you like, then not hear it again. So, as you listen, you anticipate the recurrence of that section. You feel it coming. And when it arrives, you are happy, because you like the sound, and because its familiarity gives you a sense that you are in complete control. You know exactly where you are in the music.

Repetition: The Backbone of Form

It's the listener's desire for repetition that governs the structure of every piece of music. As a result, when a composer is considering just what form a composition as a whole will take, he or she must decide which phrases or sections to repeat. Is this melody strong enough to repeat again and again? Or how about this rhythm—is it memorable, so listeners will want it to recur throughout the composition? Or is there a better one? And these harmonies—do they bear repetition or should they occur only once?

The study of large musical forms thus becomes the study of the technique of repetition. In this chapter, we'll take a look at a number of the forms that musical compositions as a whole can take, from smaller forms, like songs, to larger ones, like symphonies. We'll no longer be focusing quite as intently on the simpler elements of music, such as melodies, rhythms, and harmonies. Instead, we'll be looking at the overall structure of entire musical compositions. Our interest now is in the *form* that these compositions can take. And we shall see that the factor which, more than any other, governs this form is repetition.

Strophic Form

The simplest form that a piece of music can take on is *strophic* form. In strophic form, the same music is simply repeated over and over again. There is never any new material introduced. The melody, the rhythm, and the harmony are never changed.

Our old friend, *The Star-Spangled Banner*, is an example of strophic form. Each verse is sung to the same music. (Usually we sing only one verse, but there are a number of others.) Church hymns are the same. And so are most examples of American folk music. Think, for example, of the song, "Oh, My Darling Clementine":

1. In a cavern, in a canyon,
   Excavating for a mine,
   Dwelt a miner, forty-niner,
   And his daughter, Clementine.

2. Light she was and like a fairy,
   And her shoes were number nine,
   Herring boxes without topses,
   Sandals were for Clementine.

3. Drove she ducklings to the water
Ev'ry morning, just at nine.
Hit her foot against a splinter,
Fell into the foaming brine.

Chorus: Oh, My Darling, Oh, My Darling,
Oh, My Darling Clementine,
You are lost and gone forever,
Dreadful sorry, Clementine.

Notice that each verse, and the chorus, consists of four lines, and that the music for each line is different. The complete melody, in other words, is spread out over four lines. But when a new verse is begun, the same melody starts over again. Since we're talking about large sections now, not individual lines, we could diagram the form of "Oh, My Darling Clementine" by writing

A A A A.

This arrangement simply indicates that the song consists of four distinct sections and that each section utilizes the same music. There is no new material introduced between these sections.

For another example of strophic form, listen to an authentic blues. (The word "authentic" is used here because in recent years, the classic blues form has been treated a little carelessly by some composers.) An authentic blues consists of many verses, sometimes 15 or 20, sung to the same tune. Since the blues is a form of jazz, the performer will often improvise either words or melodies during the course of the song. But the basic structure of each verse remains the same. A ten-verse blues could be diagrammed

A A A A A A A A A A.

Variation Form

Composers of symphonic music sometimes choose a simple melody, rhythm, and harmony, and then write a composition consisting of numerous variations of these three elements. Each section of the composition is a new variation. Because the music is completely different in each section, we cannot call this strophic form. But remember that the music in each section is *based on* the same original melody, rhythm, and harmony. So we might diagram *variation form* as follows:

$$A_1 \quad A_2 \quad A_3 \quad A_4 \quad A_5 \quad A_6$$

The different numbers indicate different music in each section. The letter "A" indicates that all the variations are built on the same melody, rhythm, and harmony.

The kinds of variation that a composer might use range from simple ones to those which are extremely complicated. Simple variations could be obtained by adding a few notes to the melody, changing the rhythm slightly, or altering the instrumentation. (You might prefer thinking of a blues as being simple variation form, rather than strophic form.) In a complicated variation, the composer could, for example, split the melody in half. The first half could be played by one set of instruments. The second half could be played twice as fast and upside-down by a second set of instruments. Obviously, the only limit to variation technique is the composer's creativity.

For good examples of variation form, listen to Rachmaninoff's *Rhapsody on a Theme of Paganini*, Brahms's *Variation on a Theme by Haydn*, or any of saxophonist Charlie Parker's solos with a small combo. In each of these, the melody will first be stated by the entire orchestra or combo. In the Rachmaninoff composition, this opening statement will be followed by 23 variations. The Brahms work will consist of eight variations. The number of variations in Charlie Parker's solo will, of course, depend upon which one you listen to.

With each of these compositions, you'll have some difficulty keeping track of the original melody in the more complicated variations. But don't give up! Listen to the variations again and again. See how frequently you can spot a fragment of the basic melody, or a familiar rhythmic pattern or harmony. They might be far in the background, but they will be there, nevertheless.

Rounded Binary Form

So far, the forms we have looked at have been based on a single musical idea, repeated unchanged or in variation throughout the composition. But it's possible for a single musical idea to become tiresome. Therefore, musical forms have been developed which introduce new musical ideas at critical places in the composition. These new ideas ensure that we won't become bored with the original melody.

The most common of these forms is the *rounded binary* form. In letters, the sections of a composition in this form can be diagrammed

A A B A B A.

You can see that the new material of B is introduced after we have heard A repeated once. Thus we are allowed to take our minds away from A for a short period of time to listen to a constrasting section. But, as always, we soon desire repetition of the original idea. A enters again, followed by a repeat of B and finally section A for its fourth and last statement.

Rounded binary form solves the problem of *too much* repetition in a most satisfying manner. The most important musical idea, A, is heard four times, but not four times in a row. Instead, at two crucial points, a less important idea is introduced for variety and contrast. In the end, we remember idea A—but we're not tired of it.

Thousands of examples of rounded binary form exist. Nearly half of all popular songs which are written are in this form. In listening to any example of rounded binary form, remember each of the following points:

1. It is the *music* which repeats, not the lyrics.

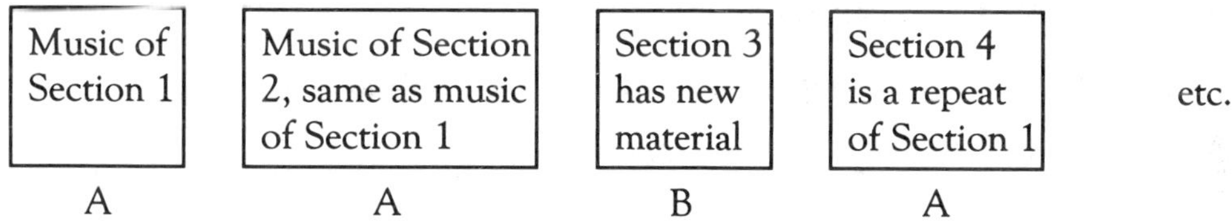

2. Sometimes the music in the third and fourth repetition of A is varied slightly. In this case, we could diagram the composition

$$A_1 \quad A_1 \quad B \quad A_2 \quad B \quad A_3.$$

3. Once in a while, some entirely new music is introduced at the end of the composition. This new material is called a *coda*. Listen to the Beatles' "Hey, Jude," and you'll hear an example of a coda after the completion of the main body of the song. (The coda takes up the last few minutes of the song and is sung to the syllables, "La, la, la . . . Hey, Jude.") Such a song can be diagrammed

A A B A B A coda.

It's not only popular songs which are written in rounded binary form. The form was also favored by composers of the late eighteenth century. Listen to any of Mozart's or Haydn's minuets. These can be heard in the first section of the third movement of any of their symphonies. Try, for example, Haydn's *Symphony No. 92*, "The Oxford," or his *Symphony No. 94*, "The Surprise"; or Mozart's *Symphony No. 41*, "The Jupiter." Another good example is the minuet of the third movement of Mozart's *Eine Kleine Nachtmusik.* Each of these minuets follows the conventional A A B A B A pattern.

Rondo Form

The technique of repetition is clearly evident in a composition written in *rondo* form. Here, a single unchanging section of musical material is alternated with a number of contrasting sections. After each section of new material, the original section is repeated again. Thus, a composition in rondo form can follow any of the following patterns:

A B A C A D A E A
or A B A C A D A
or A B A C A
or, in its simplest form, ABA.

This last, ABA, is also called *ternary* form.

Sometimes the alternating sections are themselves repeated:

A B A C A B A

or A B A B A.

A clear example of rondo form is the final movement of Beethoven's *Pathétique Sonata.* Memorize the opening melody of the movement. Then wait for this melody to reappear. Be patient! When the movement has ended, you should have heard the melody five times. And, if you have listened carefully, you should have heard other tiny musical fragments repeated throughout the piece. As an exercise, you can try to diagram the movement, using letters to represent the various melodies. Your basic pattern for the rondo will be

A __ A __ A __ A __ A.

Your job is to fill in the blanks with letters B, C, D, etc. Notice that each blank might contain two or three or more letters to indicate two or three or more musical fragments.

The exercise is a difficult one. You'll have to listen to the *Pathétique* many times to carry it out successfully, but you'll be well rewarded. The music will no

longer be a meaningless jumble of sound. It will have order to it. It will suddenly make sense. You'll see that Beethoven had a plan. By getting *inside* the music and unscrambling the repetitions of rondo form, you will have gained satisfying insight into a difficult piece of music.

Sonata Form

During the mid-eighteenth century, one of classical music's most durable musical forms developed. It became the most important form of the next 50 years, utilized many times by Haydn, Mozart, Beethoven, and Schubert. Later composers continued to find it useful and even today, more than 200 years later, this form governs the structure of many contemporary compositions. It's called *sonata* form.

A composition written in sonata form usually is based on two melodies of equal importance. These melodies are called *themes*. The composition opens with a playing of the first theme. This is followed by a connecting passage, or *bridge*, to the second theme. The playing of the second theme marks the end of the first section of the composition. This first section is called the *exposition.*

The exposition is followed by the *development* section. If you'll think back to some of the techniques of variation form, you'll have an idea of how the two themes are treated here. They are taken apart by the composer and then expanded upon. The composer changes instrumentation, puts the two themes together, disguises them, adds to them, rearranges them. In short, the composer's job in the development section is to create new and interesting music which is *based on* the two original themes.

The development is followed by the *recapitulation* section. Here the two themes are re-stated in their original form, one at a time. Sometimes the composition will end here, or sometimes it will be followed by a coda. The coda is no different in theory from the coda of "Hey, Jude." It consists of some new material, or perhaps a reworking of a few ideas from the development. With the coda, the composition is ended.

If we label the exposition "E," the development "D," and the recapitulation "R," we obtain the following diagram for a composition in sonata form:

E D R
or possibly E D R + coda.

If we take into consideration the fact that the exposition is sometimes repeated, and that the development-recapitulation sequence is also sometimes repeated, we derive a few more possible diagrams:

E E D R *or* E E D R + coda
or E E D R D R *or* E E D R D R + coda.

With sonata form, we are once again made aware of the importance of repetition. We hear the principal themes stated in both the exposition and the recapitulation. And further, we hear those themes, in fragmented form, in the development. Because they are fragmented in this middle section, we might think of the development as the "intellectual" section. Here we have to be on our toes. We must call up all of our skill as listeners to determine what the composer has done with the themes. In the development more than in the exposition or recapitulation, we have to work to keep track of what is going on.

To test your ability to pick out the sections of a composition written in sonata form, listen to the first movement of Beethoven's lovely "Archduke" *Trio.* The trio is written for three instruments—a piano, a violin, and a cello. The opening theme is a lyrical melody played first by the piano and then, after a bridge passage, by the strings. Don't be impatient for the beginning of the second theme, for there will be some transitional music before its entrance. You'll recognize the second theme as a crisp, descending melody, entirely different in character from the first theme. It will be played first by the piano alone, then by the strings. After passing among the three instruments for a short period of time, the second theme and the exposition will come to an end.

Now, if you have a completely accurate recording of the "Archduke," the exposition will be repeated in its entirety. You'll be able to spot this easily, for the first theme will enter again on the piano, exactly as you heard it the first time. The exposition will now continue without change.

In the development, you should be able to spot fragments of the two themes drifting around among the three instruments. All of the music that you hear in this section will be related to themes. But don't worry if you can't decipher all of the relationships. And don't panic if you temporarily lose track of the principal melodies. Enjoy yourself while you're looking for thematic fragments.

You'll know the development is coming to an end when you hear the violinist and cellist playing "pizzicato," that is, by plucking the strings rather than bowing them. The first theme will then enter again on the piano, signaling the beginning of the recapitulation. You'll hear the second theme again and, at last, a short coda. Playing together briskly, the three instruments will bring the coda, and the movement itself, to an end.

An Important Distinction

You may have noticed that we have used the word "sonata" in two ways in this chapter. First you listened to an example of rondo form in Beethoven's *Pathétique Sonata.* Then you looked closely at "sonata" form in the "Archduke" *Trio.* This suggests that there is an important distinction to be made in the two uses of the word. The first "sonata" (the *Pathétique*) is a *type* of composition for piano, or for a solo instrument with piano accompaniment. It is made up of three or four smaller compositions called *movements.* You listened to the fourth and final movement of the *Pathétique.* This kind of sonata, then, is a collection of movements.

On the other hand, "sonata" form refers to just *single* movements. You studied sonata form in the first movement of the "Archduke" *Trio.* The structure of the movement was based on sonata form. So *a* sonata is made up of movements, some of which may be in variation form, some in rondo form, or some, in fact, in sonata form. And sonata *form* may describe the structure of a movement from a symphony, a trio, a string quartet, or indeed a sonata.

Larger Forms

Finally, let's take a look at some of the larger forms of classical music, to describe in general terms some of the words we have been casually throwing around. We'll investigate briefly the five most important, large musical forms—the symphony, the concerto, the string quartet, the trio, and the sonata.

Consider first the following generalizations about the five forms:

1. All are divided into smaller "compositions" called movements.
2. Each normally consists of three or four movements.
3. Each movement has its own special form, often one of the forms you've studied (variation form, rondo form, and sonata form).
4. In the works of Haydn, Mozart, Beethoven, Schubert, and many other composers, the following pattern holds true for four-movement compositions:
   - The first movement is usually in sonata form.
   - The second movement is usually in sonata form, variation form, or ternary form.
   - The third movement is usually in ternary form.
   - The fourth movement is usually in sonata form or rondo form.
5. The movements contrast with each other in speed and character. A general pattern for four-movement compositions is fast and exciting first and fourth movements; a slow, emotional second movement; and a gentle, dance-like third movement.
6. The movements contrast with each other in meter. Often the first, second, and fourth movements are in duple meter, the third movement in triple meter.

Now, by means of the following chart, study the instrumentation of the five large forms:

Symphony	**Concerto**	**String Quartet**	**Trio**	**Sonata**
Played by an entire orchestra	Played by an entire orchestra but featuring a soloist, usually a pianist or a violinist	Played by two violins, a viola, and a cello	Played by three instruments, usually piano, violin, and cello	Played by piano alone, or a solo instrument, such as violin or cello, with piano accompaniment

Of course there are exceptions to all of the generalizations that we've made. Beginning in the late nineteenth century, the exceptions came more and more frequently. For example, Gustav Mahler wrote a number of symphonies which contained more than four movements. Tchaikovsky wrote a movement (the second movement of his *Sixth Symphony*) in quintuple meter. But by and large, you'll be safe assuming that the generalizations are true. And to see how well they work, you should listen to as many classical compositions as you can. Try two or three Haydn or Mozart symphonies. Then listen to another Beethoven sonata and a Schubert string quartet. As you listen, keep your list of generalizations handy. See how well the list describes each of the compositions that you study.

Form, Then, Brings Order

This chapter should have helped you to see that a great deal of reasoning goes into the construction of a large musical work. The final product isn't just a meaningless bundle of sounds. It has order—order which is guaranteed by the composer's skillful use of form. Form gives the composer a foundation on which to build the entire composition.

STUDY ACTIVITIES

1. You've studied five different musical forms in this chapter. A certain mad composer always combines *three* of these forms in his compositions. The combinations which he chooses vary from composition to composition. Tell which combinations he has used if each of the following diagrams represent the pattern of repetition in one of his compositions:

   a. A_1 B A_1 C A_1 D A_1 A_1 A_1 A_1 A_2 A_3 A_4

   ____________, ____________, and ____________

   b. A_1 A_1 B A_1 B A_1 B C B D_1 D_2 D_3

   ____________, ____________, and ____________

   c. E E D R_1 D R_1 R_1 R_1 S R_1 M R_1

   ____________, ____________, and ____________

   d. (A little harder!) G G G P G P G

   ____________, ____________, and ____________

2. One possible pattern for sonata form is E E D R D R. Can you see any similarity between this pattern and the pattern of repetition present in a rounded binary form composition? If so, what is the similarity?

3. Suppose that a person who knows nothing about music sits down at a piano and begins "playing." A friend tape-records the resulting five-minute composition and later plays it back for you. What weaknesses in the composition might you be able to spot?

4. If you listened to the second movement of a typical Mozart symphony, and then followed it with the third movement of a typical Haydn string quartet, what differences between the two movements would you notice? You should be able to list at least five significant differences.

5. You are a composer writing a four-section composition. Two of those sections will be the same, the third and fourth will be different. Thus, you have two A's, a B, and a C to work with. What would be the best pattern in which to arrange your A, A, B, and C? Why? (Remember, a composer has freedom to do as he or she wishes. Therefore, there's no correct or incorrect answer to this question. Just be certain that you can justify the particular arrangement of letters which you choose.)

6. Again, as in 5, you are a composer, this time working on a six-section composition. The letters you have to work with are A, A, A, B, B, and C. What is the best arrangement? Why?

Chapter 7

CONTENT

In Chapter 1, you saw that there was a distinct difference between art and music with respect to the effort that we must exert to enjoy them. Art, to be enjoyed, has to be looked at. Music, on the other hand, to be enjoyed does not have to be listened to. Music can drift through the air and be heard but not actually perceived. To understand music, we saw that we have to be active participants in the experience. Understanding requires work.

Music and art can also differ in a second and unrelated way if the art happens to be realistic rather than abstract. Suppose you are viewing a painting by Rembrandt, El Greco, or another of the great realist painters. How can you tell what the painting is about? Easy! You just look at it! The subject of the painting is obvious. It might be a landscape or a still life or a portrait or a battle scene, but whatever it is, we immediately know the subject the artist is commenting upon. The picture we see has relevance to our everyday experience. Shapes, lines, and colors all can be easily associated in our minds with specific objects and ideas.

But with music, meaning is not at all clear. Rhythms don't represent trees and flowers, harmonies are not battleships. The themes of a symphony have no relevance to our everyday experience as do the shapes of a painting. In music we can't "see" what a composer is trying to say in a composition.

. . . Which Raises Some Interesting Questions

How, then, can we assign meaning to abstract quantities like notes and melodies? Or more generally, just what does music mean?

Our search for answers to these questions will certainly be the most difficult we have yet undertaken. Let's begin by recalling two words that were introduced in Chapter 4: consonance and dissonance. We noted that there were some sounds which we interpreted as "pleasing." They had an enjoyable quality which we liked listening to. We called such sounds "consonances." Other sounds, however, were not so pleasing. Much modern music is filled with these sounds, with the result that many people totally reject this music. It is dissonant music. Something about it simply makes people shudder.

But we made an interesting observation about consonance and dissonance. The dedicated and open-minded listener soon finds that dissonance can become consonance. The listener makes the remarkable discovery that there is nothing *basically* wrong with dissonance. In other words, it wasn't an inherent characteristic which made certain sounds seem dissonant.

But what was it?

The answer is that it was *acquired knowledge*. We aren't born with a mechanism which forces us to accept some sounds and reject others. We *learn* to do this. We grow up with sounds of a certain kind and grow to like those sounds. So when we suddenly run into unusual harmonies, they seem strange because they are new. We label them "dissonant."

The clearest proof of this fact is the experience of Western listeners hearing Asian music for the first time. Everything about this music—the instruments, the melodies, the harmonies—is new to the listener. And few Westerners can honestly say that they like what they hear. Yet people who live in countries where this music is common find it to be quite agreeable. It sounds natural to them for they have heard it all their lives.

We conclude that music itself is neither consonant nor dissonant. These words are simply labels pinned on music by listeners for convenience, or perhaps for identification purposes. In large part, they are a measure of one's total musical experience; for the greater one's experience, the less use one finds for the concept of dissonance.

But Weren't We Talking About "Meaning"?

So what does this have to do with "meaning" in music? Only that, beyond what we have observed concerning consonance and dissonance specifically, we have seen that it is possible to *learn* to make real and meaningful interpretations of essentially abstract music. We learn as children to think of some sounds as dissonant and therefore unpleasant, or even "bad." We learn that a certain slow kind of music is "mournful." We learn that high, fast music played by violins is "happy." We learn that a meandering bassoon solo is "funny." Specific sounds in music come to have meaning for us because of the associations we have learned to make. And we apply adjectives like "mournful," "happy," and "funny" to certain kinds of music, music which, without our learning, would be none of these things.

Thus, some kinds of music can actually have immediate relevance to our everyday experience. They can produce general emotions, such as "sadness" or "happiness," which are very real to us. Some composers, capitalizing on this fact and using orchestration imaginatively, can also give us glimpses of *specific* objects and events. Music of this kind is called *program music.* Its purpose is to portray for us an actual event or experience as accurately as possible. The composer tries to paint in our minds a picture as full of reality as any painting which hangs in an art museum. Tchaikovsky's *1812 Overture,* for example, is a depiction of an actual event, Napoleon's defeat in Russia in the year 1812. Berlioz's *Symphonie Fantastique* shows us country scenes, dreams, witches, a funeral, even a depressing march to the gallows. Honegger's *Pacific 231* is the composer's impression of a train in motion. And Sibelius's *Finlandia* is a portrait of the composer's homeland. These works, and many others like them, aren't just abstract music. They are attempts to depict actual scenes which lie outside of music.

Can We Always Guess the Meaning of Program Music?

Program music, unfortunately, has a weakness. Sometimes we don't know what a composer is talking about *until we are told.* Berlioz, for example, wrote a long description of his *Symphonie Fantastique* for listeners to read. Here's one of the sentences from the description: "He sees his beloved at a dance, in the midst of the tumult of an exciting festival." If we read this and then listen to the music, we say: "Ah, yes, I can see everything Berlioz wanted me to see." But would we have understood these details from the symphony if we *hadn't* read the composer's description? Probably not. Music simply isn't capable of calling to our minds the image of a man seeing his beloved at a dance. Only if we are first told that this is what we are supposed to see will we see it.

In many of his operas, the German composer Richard Wagner used a tactic similar to Berlioz's written description, but slightly more subtle. Wagner assigned a short melody called a *leitmotiv* to each of the characters in his operas. When one of the characters appears onstage, the orchestra plays the appropriate *leitmotiv*. Soon audiences learn to associate each *leitmotiv* with a particular character. They are "trained" to see that character whenever they hear his or her personal melody. Thus, later in the opera, even when the character isn't onstage, the playing of the *leitmotiv* makes the audience "see" the character.

Wagner has done exactly what Berlioz did. He has *told* us the meaning of each *leitmotiv*. We associate each character with a theme because we have seen and heard the two together so many times. Without learning what Wagner intended us to learn, his *leitmotivs* would have no meaning.

Content

Our findings so far can be summarized in one simple statement: The content of a piece of music can be taught to the listener.

Content is simply the meaning and feeling contained in a musical composition. It doesn't exist in black and white, like notes, or in waves, like melodies. Instead, it's an abstract quality, a quality which conveys ideas and emotions. The summarizing statement above points out our surprising finding that this abstract quality, content, can actually be *forced* on a listener. We have seen two ways in which this can happen.

1. Years of listening to music can teach us that certain sounds are "unpleasant" or dissonant and certain sounds are "sad" while others are "happy" or "funny." We noted that, especially in the case of dissonance, it's possible for dedicated listeners to change their ideas about the content of such sounds.

2. The composer can teach the content of a piece of music to the audience. We saw this done in program music, where the composer told the listener specifically what the music was about.

Possibly by this time, you're feeling a little disappointed. It seems as though we're going to have to be forced to accept specific content in music. But let's reconsider. There appears to be a certain weakness in the kinds of music we have investigated so far. Berlioz's *Symphonie Fantastique* works all right—as long as we're willing to accept his written description of the content of the symphony. Wagner's *leitmotivs* work all right—as long as we're willing to accept the training he gives us through the repetition of visual images on the stage. And music which imitates such sounds from life as bells, thunder, and railroad trains, works all right—as long as we're willing to put up with tricks of orchestration when we could be listening to the real thing! But most listeners aren't willing to do any of these things. And why should they? After all, blind acceptance of content takes away a listener's most valuable possession—the freedom to interpret music as one wishes. Without Berlioz's description, you might have heard something entirely different in the *Symphonie Fantastique*. Would there be anything wrong with that? And how long can we remain interested in music which imitates bells and thunder and railroad trains? A short time, probably, and then we'll become bored.

All of these factors help to explain why program music enjoyed popularity for only a relatively short period of time in music history. Audiences simply didn't want to be told what a particular composition was about. They preferred to exercise their freedom to interpret music as they wished. And you should feel the same way. If someone, or some piece of writing, tells you that a particular piece of music is about a storm, for example, you should feel insulted. You'll realize that for one specific person, or perhaps for the composer of the composition, the music may be about a storm. But for you, the music is about whatever you want it to be. Because music is abstract, its content will vary from listener to listener. No one can tell you what that content is.

But Isn't the Composer Telling Us Something?

The meaning of a piece of music is thus a very personal matter. People who don't realize this often become terribly confused about the concept of "communication" in music. Such people assume that a composer is trying to communicate something to listeners. Perhaps it is an emotion, or impressions of an event, or possibly even some complex message about the importance of certain values in life. Whatever it is, these people spend a great deal of time trying to discover just what it was that the composer was attempting to communicate. But as you have seen, music is an abstract art. It simply can't do a very good job of communicating specific ideas. Any composer with a message for listeners will do much better to write it out, as Berlioz did, or else use the telephone! People who search for the content intended by a composer are wasting their time. The only message that composers can possibly convey through their music is the one which says that they love to create, and that this love causes them to compose music.

So we are left with a fact which might be difficult for you to accept: Music has *no* meaning except the meaning which you assign to it. By itself, music is meaningless. The greatest orchestra in the world playing for an empty concert hall is playing meaningless music. There must be listeners. And listeners have the freedom to interpret music as they choose. No one can tell them what the music is about. Its content is up to them.

So How Does One Determine Content?

As a listener you have two choices in determining the content of a piece of music. First of all you can interpret it in terms borrowed from your everyday life. You can call it "sad," if you wish, or "happy," or "energetic," or whatever emotion the music seems to inspire in you. You have seen how reactions of this kind are actually learned reactions. They are based on your total experience in music and, like all interpretations, they will vary from listener to listener.

You can carry this method of determining content further and actually incorporate your emotions into a story. There's nothing wrong with your viewing a movement from a particular symphony as a storm, for example, if that seems appropriate. Remember only that this is your own personal interpretation. Don't force it on anyone else. Let this interpretation make the symphony more meaningful for you. But be prepared to make slight changes in your interpretation each time that you listen to the composition. For just as the content of a piece of music changes from listener to listener, so it can change for a specific individual each time he or she listens to that piece of music. This is part of the magic of good music—it never stands still. It is always changing.

A second method of determining content in music might be more difficult for you to use, but in many ways you'll find it far more satisfying than the first method. Neglect specific adjectives like "sad" or "exciting." Avoid interpreting music as a story. Simply accept music as the abstract art that it is. And give it abstract meaning. Convince yourself that *music expresses nothing but itself.* It has no concrete meaning. Music is sound—sound arranged in a particular way by a composer, to be sure—but nonetheless nothing but sound. It reaches your ears and causes you to think. You enjoy it, not because it is "happy," not because it might depict a storm, but simply because it is music. When you accept this seemingly obvious fact, you suddenly become aware of the reason that music has always cast a spell over humans: music is wonderful because it is music.

Finally, consider one last reason for accepting music abstractly. If you don't burden yourself with the chore of assigning a specific story line to a composition, you'll have far more time to investigate the details of the composition. You'll be able to listen closely to melody and rhythm. You'll see how the composer has built themes from notes, and movements from themes, and finally, symphonies from movements. You'll be able to get inside the composition to see relationships which otherwise you might have missed. And finally, you'll see that music really *is* abstract and that the only way to accept it is on its own terms.

Study Activities

1. The text mentioned four pieces of program music: Tchaikovsky's *1812 Overture*, Berlioz's *Symphonie Fantastique*, Honegger's *Pacific 231*, and Sibelius's *Finlandia*. Choose one of these compositions and read a description of what the music is supposed to depict. Then listen to a recording of the composition. Afterwards, answer the following questions.
   a. How well did the music depict what the composer wanted it to depict?
   b. In what specific ways did the composer make you "see" what he was trying to depict?
   c. Suppose you hadn't first read a description of the music. Would you have guessed any of the images the composer was attempting to show? Which ones?

2. When we listen to a popular song, we assume that the song is "about" what the lyrics say it is about. But is it possible for the content of a popular song to be *different* from the content of the lyrics? In other words, can the music itself dictate the content?

3. In the Study Activities following Chapter 1, you answered a question concerning a teenager who had never heard music before his fifteenth birthday. Go back to that question (question 3, page 5) and see if you would answer it any differently now in light of what you've learned since Chapter 1.

4. Listen to Debussy's *La Mer*. Try to neglect the fact that for Debussy, the composition was about the sea. What is it for you? Write a paragraph or two describing what the music means to you.

Chapter 8

MAKING MUSIC

Suppose you were a composer and were told to create a piece of music using just 12 tones. Could you do it?

The answer is that not only could you do it, you could create every symphony Beethoven ever wrote, every song the Beatles ever performed, every opera Wagner ever composed. In fact, you could create practically every piece of music written in the history of Western music, for nearly all have been composed of combinations and variations of just 12 basic tones.

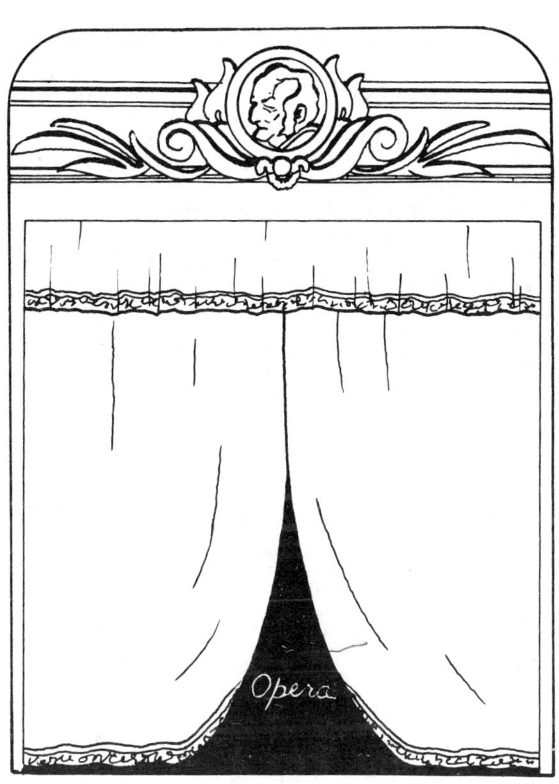

Start With the Notes

Here is how the 12 tones, or notes, appear in musical notation. Their names are written beneath the notes.

The five lines on which the notes are written are called a *staff*. Learning to read music consists of learning to associate the notes written on a staff with the actual musical tones that they represent, and then singing those tones or playing them on an instrument.

Reading music is not as difficult as many people think. Perhaps you already know how; if not, this chapter will teach you the basics. Consider continuing your study in order to become even more adept at reading music. With this additional skill in your repertoire, you're certain to find it adding to both your enjoyment and your understanding of music.

The symbol 𝄞 which appears at the beginning of the staff is called the G-clef. Notice how the "curl" in the clef wraps around the line on which the note G appears. This identifies the position of G, providing a fixed point from which the positions of all the other notes can be measured.

Just as ideas can be explained using different words, so musical tones can be given different names. Thus, instead of the name C#, for example, the fifth note illustrated on page 65 can also be called D♭ and written

Although it is notated differently, the note D♭ sounds exactly the same as the note C#.

Above and below the 12 basic notes there are others, but all are variations of the 12 fundamental notes. Here is how the variations are achieved: When the frequency of a tone doubles (that is, when the number of times that the sound wave vibrates each second doubles), a different note that sounds similar to the first is produced. Since it sounds like the first it is given the same name (A, D, F#, and so on). The new note is said to be one *octave* higher than the first. Sing the words "say" and "see" in the first line of the *Star-Spangled Banner*, and you'll hear two notes that are one octave apart.

Can you hear the similarity in the two tones? Although the second one is "higher," it has a quality that makes it sound like the first.

Since the note that the word "say" is sung to is written on the line labeled C in the note-identification staff, the note to which "see" is sung to must also be C. If you could measure the frequency of your vocal chords as you sang the word "see," you would find that they were vibrating twice as fast as they were when you sang "say." If you were to double the frequency again, you would produce an even higher octave, and another note called C that sounded like the first two.

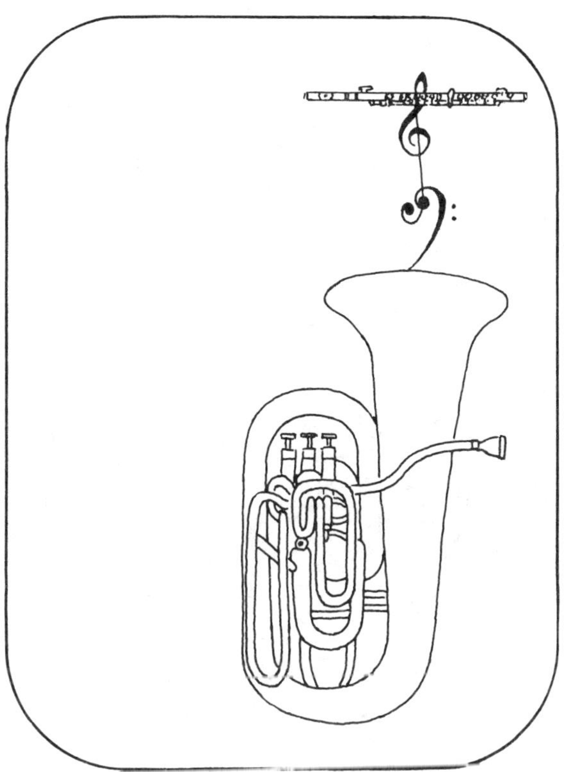

Now you can see how the 12-note foundation that a composer works with is enlarged through octave variations. Each note that can be produced by any instrument, from the lowest note on a tuba to the highest note on a piccolo, is simply a version of one of the basic 12. If it is not one of the 12 itself, it can be created from one by doubling (or halving) its frequency one or more times. In this way whole families of A's, G's, C#'s, and so on are created.

You can see how all of this fits together by studying the keyboard of a piano. There are 88 keys on a piano, each producing a single note. The entire keyboard is divided into seven octaves plus four extra notes which begin an eighth octave ([7 x 12] + 4 = 84 + 4 = 88). There are seven notes called G on a piano. Since one of the extra notes is an A, there are *eight* notes called A on a piano. The frequencies of the sound waves producing the A sounds range from the lowest at 27½ vibrations per second to the highest at 3,520 vibrations per second. Each higher A is created by doubling the frequency of a lower A.

A 27½ × 2 = A 55 × 2 = A 110 × 2 = A 220 × 2 = A 440 × 2 = A 880 × 2 = A 1760 × 2 = A 3520

Now, Add the Rhythm

A composer can further vary the music produced by the 12 basic notes by varying the lengths of time that the various notes sound. You'll recall from

Chapter 3 that these varying lengths produce the *rhythm* of a piece of music. On paper, the length of time that a note is meant to be played or sung is indicated by the "head," "stem," and "tail" of the note:

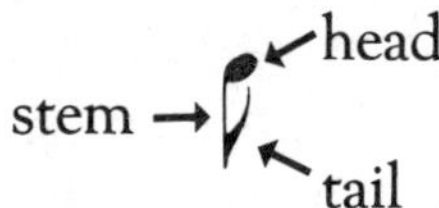

Note							
Head	open	open	closed	closed	closed	closed	closed
Stem	none	one	one	one	one	one	one
Tail	none	none	none	one	two	three	four
Name	whole note	half note	quarter note	eighth note	sixteenth note	thirty-second note	sixty-fourth note

Each of these notes has a duration exactly half that of the previous note. Thus, two half notes can be played in the same amount of time that it takes to play a whole note ($2 \times \frac{1}{2} = 1$). Four sixteenth notes can be played in the same amount of time it takes to play a quarter note or two eighth notes ($4 \times \frac{1}{16} = 1 \times \frac{1}{4} = 2 \times \frac{1}{8}$).

With the rhythm indicated, here is how the first line of the *Star-Spangled Banner* appears on paper.

The vertical marks between notes are called *bar lines*. They divide the music into *measures*, each of them three quarter notes (or their equivalent) in duration. The steady pulse which keeps the song moving is a repeating pattern of three beats.

One-two-three
One-two-three

Oh, --	say can you --	see --- by the	dawn's ear-ly ---	light . . .
One two three	One two three	One two three	One two three	One . . .

The measures carve the song into three-beat divisions.

Sing the line several times and notice how you sing the eighth notes ("Oh" and "by the") twice as fast as you sing the quarter notes, and how you linger on the half notes ("see" and "light") twice as long as you linger on the quarter notes. These variations produce the characteristic rhythm of the song. By using the same melody but changing the rhythm, you could compose a song with an entirely different character. That is the special quality that rhythm imparts to music.

. . . The Rests . . .

Sometimes what is not played is as important as what is played in a piece of music. A "rest" is used to indicate silence in musical notation. Like notes, rests vary in length from the "whole" variety to "sixty-fourths."

whole half quarter eighth sixteenth thirty-second sixty-fourth

A rest tells a performer *not* to play or sing during the period of time indicated by the rest.

. . . The Harmony and the Form

Next, a composer will stack groups of notes into chords to produce the harmonies that you studied in Chapter 4, and decide how to divide melodies up among the various instruments. Finally, the composer will organize all of this into a form that is appropriate to his or her conception of the music.

On the following page you will find the first page of the *Requiem Mass*, church music for voices and orchestra. The composition was begun by Wolfgang Amadeus Mozart, and completed by Franz Xaver Süssmayr after Mozart's death.

So here is a major work of music on paper. The word *Adagio* near the top is an Italian term which tells the conductor that the music should be performed at slow speed. The instruments and voices for which Mozart scored the piece are listed at the left, beside the staffs carrying their music. Although the instrument names are in Italian, those for timpani, violin, viola, cello, and organ are easily recognized. "Corni di Bassetto" means "basset horn," a type of clarinet. "Fagotti" means "bassoons," and "Trombe" means "trumpets."

You'll see that most of the staffs begin with a G clef, fixing the note G on the second line from the bottom. But two other types of clef appear as well. The staffs for the bassoon, the timpani, the cellos, the organ, and the bass voice begin with F clefs. The curl fixes the note F on the second line from the top. The viola uses a C clef, which fixes the note C in the middle of the staff. These departures from the use of the more conventional G clef occur because the comfortable playing range for these instruments is different from that of the G-clef instruments. So that most of the notes written for them will appear *on* the staff rather than above or below it, different positions are chosen for their fixed notes.

You'll also see that staffs of the singers and some instruments have no notes. Instead they have rest marks, which mean that their parts are silent during the opening of the composition.

To indicate the beat of a piece of music, the composer must furnish a *time signature*. Many different time signatures are possible; here, Mozart uses the traditional symbol 𝄴 . It indicates that he has chosen the quarter note as his standard for a single beat, and that there will be four such beats in every measure.

Beneath the first note of every staff you'll see the letter *p*. This is an abbreviation for *piano*, meaning soft, the volume at which Mozart wants performers to begin the piece. Many other instructions about volume are found later in the *Requiem*.

All of the notes and symbols and directions on this page are needed to tell the performers what to do in the first several seconds of the piece. The entire score includes 104 pages with many thousands of symbols. Major scores like this can be extremely complex, containing several hours worth of music featuring more than 100 performers.

And Play!

Composers write music for countless numbers and configurations of performers, from soloists to the hundreds that are needed to perform an opera or a complex symphony like Gustav Mahler's *Symphony No. 8*, the "Symphony of a Thousand." Now that you have studied the basics of how a piece of music is put together, listen to some of these arrangements, begining with a solo performance and working your way slowly forward to compositions of great complexity. The Listening List for Chapter 8 suggests some performances you will probably enjoy. As you listen, imagine how the composer might have put each work together, choosing melodies and rhythms, deciding what form the piece would take and what performers it would be written for. This should be relatively easy with the solo performance. As you work your way through duets, trios, and beyond, adding layer upon layer of complexity, the challenge will increase with each step. Try to hear how the layers of even the largest works have been constructed of the same elements that comprise the smallest. Listen to how the melodies interweave and how the rhythms give character to a work. And always keep in mind the 12 basic notes, the building blocks from which all of this music has been created.

Study Activities

1. A certain note has a frequency of 600 vibrations per second. Find the frequencies of the notes one, two, and three octaves above this note, and one, two, and three octaves below.
2. The highest note called B on a piano has a frequency of 1,984 vibrations per second. What is the frequency of the lowest B on a piano?
3. How many sixteenth notes can be played in the amount of time it takes to play a whole note?
4. How many eighth notes can be played in the amount of time it takes to play a half note?
5. How many sixty-fourth rests are equivalent to four quarter rests?
6. Hum the same melody but change the rhythm of the first line of *The Star-Spangled Banner.* Try to do this in several different ways. Why might it be harder to do this than it would be to create a rhythm for a melody you are making up yourself?
7. In writing music for the lyrics to a song, why might a composer decide to set one word to a whole note and another word to a sixteenth or thirty-second note?

Chapter 9

NEW MUSIC

Throughout most of the history of Western music, composers of classical music have found large and enthusiastic audiences for their works. Even in the most unconventional compositions, listeners have found some element of the music they could enjoy—hummable melodies, exciting rhythms, beautiful and provocative harmonies. As music evolved into more and more complex forms, audiences evolved too, bringing an ever-deeper level of sophistication to even the most controversial pieces. Occasionally a composer or piece of music was judged too radical and suffered rejection for a time. (At the premier of Igor Stravinksy's *Rite of Spring* in 1913, a huge uproar erupted in the audience, with some listeners shouting "Genius!" while others bellowed with equal vehemence, "Fraud!" Fistfights broke out, members of the orchestra were attacked, and the composer himself was forced to flee the theater through a backstage window.) But almost always, even pieces such as these have slowly grown to seem commonplace and have gained acceptance by audiences. Today, Stravinsky's *Rite of Spring* is one of the most frequently performed—and most beloved—compositions in the classical repertoire.

All of this has changed dramatically during the past quarter-century. Beginning in the years following World War II and escalating during the 1960's and 1970's, many composers of classical music have made clean breaks with the melodic, rhythmic, and harmonic traditions of the past. Tired of conventional sounds, believing that many of the assumptions about how music should be written and performed had outlived their usefulness, composers have begun a search for radically different sounds. The result is a kind of music that for lack of a better term we might call "new music." In jazz, too, a host of performers have broken with tradition and begun playing their own brand of "new music," free improvisation that is no less revolutionary than the new classical music.

One of the consequences of these developments is that, for the first time, serious listeners have almost unanimously abandoned contemporary classical music and jazz. New music has found only the tiniest of audiences. The majority of listeners who in the past evolved along with even the most experimental music, and gradually accepted it, have gone elsewhere in their search for listening enjoyment.

A Crisis—And a Challenge

Composers and performers of new music are no less talented or sincere than their predecessors have been. But because of the radically different nature of new music, audiences have by and large been unwilling to accept it. Most new works, no matter how worthy, are performed only a few times and then never heard again. This crisis in the relationship between composer and audience is unprecedented in the entire history of music. And yet no matter how alarming this development may be, it presents you, the listener, with a unique and exciting challenge. A huge body of generally unappreciated music, written and performed by some of the greatest musical talents of our time, awaits you. Coming to terms with it, learning to enjoy it, will require effort and all of your listening skills. The rewards, as always, will justify the effort, for you will have opened yourself to a whole spectrum of new musical experiences. That is what listening is all about.

Getting Started—Again

Listening to new music is like starting all over again. Whatever preconceptions you may have about how serious music is supposed to sound, you may find yourself unprepared for new music. You may even decide that it isn't music! Spend some time listening to works by one or two of the composers listed in the Listening List for Chapter 9. The music may sound chaotic or disorganized to you. You probably won't hear any hummable melodies or familiar harmonies. More likely you'll hear what one critic has characterized as "honks, squeaks, blips, blasts, screams, ouches, and the death rattle of an expiring vacuum cleaner."

That was not written in jest. Some new music produces precisely such sounds. The music in Robert Moran's *39 Minutes for 39 Autos* is created by synthesizers, airplanes, and—yes—39 automobile horns. To perform *Portable Gold and Philosophers' Stones*, composer David Rosenboom wires the heads of his "performers" with electrodes; the music is produced by the performers' brainwaves. John Cage, one of the first of the new composers and probably the most influential, wrote a piece called *4′33″* which called for the performers to sit in complete silence throughout the entire composition. His work *0′0″* he performed solo by slicing, dicing, and puréeing a grocery bag full of vegetables, then drinking the resulting concoction. Amplifiers broadcast the sound of his drinking and swallowing to the audience.

Is this music? Audiences who are used to Beethoven and Brahms say no. New composers argue that music is organized sound, and that it makes no less sense to organize the sound of car horns or puréeing vegetables into a musical experience than it does to organize the sound of violins and French horns into a symphony. There is only one way for you, the listener, to decide, and that is to open your mind and your ears to the sound of new music. Listen diligently, giving it its best chance to prove itself. Then and only then are you equipped to render an informed decision.

A Little History

The movement away from traditional sounds actually began early in the twentieth century, when a few composers began to feel enslaved by the constraints of traditional composing techniques. The rules of how music should sound restricted their freedom, and they began to search for ways to compose music that were not dependent on *tonal centers*—the requirement that all tones and chords in a piece of music relate to a single keynote. (In the first line of *The Star-Spangled Banner*, the note to which the word "say" is sung is never far away throughout the piece. The melody and harmony of the song are built around that note and return to it again and again. Nearly all Western music written before the twentieth century also is composed in reference to a single note.)

In an effort to overcome these restraints, the Austrian composer Arnold Schönberg created a new method of composition called the 12-tone system. Schönberg's system placed equal emphasis on all of the 12 basic notes of music. By mathematically balancing all notes, he created music that was devoid of a tonal center.

Not surprisingly, Schönberg's "atonal" music proved disorienting to audiences. The traditional underlying structure of music was gone. In its place was a new system which produced music that seemed aimless, random—totally lacking in structure. Of course, the structure was there—Schönberg was an extremely talented and experienced composer—but it was so unconventional that audiences couldn't find it. Thus began the disillusionment of listeners with new music. Like any true artist, Schönberg wanted to explore new territory. He succeeded, but in so doing, he alienated much of his audience.

Listen to Schönberg's *String Quartet in D Minor* or his *Five Piano Pieces*, or to any of the music by his disciple Anton von Webern. Instead of judging at once, or trying to relate the music to what you have heard before, listen to it as pure sound. Experience the music emotionally, enjoy the variety of the rhythms, the surprises that await you at each turn. You'll notice the absence of a tonal center, but instead of treating that as a drawback, try to hear it for what Schönberg intended it to be: a casting aside of antiquated limits, an opening up of a new and exciting frontier in music.

New Rhythms and Harmonies

Schönberg liberated music tonally. Other composers have felt as constrained as Schönberg felt but have laid the blame on traditional Western rhythms and harmonies. Some, like Alan Hovhaness, George Crumb, and Lou Harrison, have turned to Asian, Indian, Persian, and other exotic traditions in a search for new sounds. For a good introduction to this kind of music, listen to the non-Western sounds of Hovhaness's *Khaldis Concerto for Piano, Four Trumpets, and Percussion*, his

Lousadzak Concerto for Piano and Strings, or his *Talin.* Crumb's *Haunted Landscape* is scored for 45 different percussion instruments, including Cambodian *angklungs,* Japanese *kabuki* blocks, a Brazilian *cuica,* Caribbean steel drums, and an Appalachian hammered dulcimer. Harrison has experimented extensively with Eastern sonorities and rhythms. To ears accustomed to Western music, the half step you sing to the words "home of" in the last line of *The Star-Spangled Banner* ("and the *home of* the brave") seems to be the smallest melodic step possible. Harrison routinely carves melodies into quarter-tones, eighth-tones, and other "micro" tones. He has used Korean scales, Mongolian folk music, medieval rhythms, and ancient Babylonian scales in his music. Listen to his *Three Pieces for Gamelan,* the *Double Concerto for Violin, Cello, and Javanese Gamelan,* or *At the Tomb of Charles Ives.*

For an entirely different approach to exotic sounds, listen to the homemade instruments (the cloudchamber bowl and the *quadrangularis reversum* are two) of Harry Partch. Partch invented these instruments because, quite simply, no others were capable of playing the 43-note-to-the-octave scale that his compositions required. (Recall that traditional Western music has 12 notes to the octave.)

Electronic Music

Perhaps the greatest boon to composers seeking new horizons in music has been the invention of electronic instruments and techniques of sound manipulation. This began in the 1950's with compositions like Edward Varese's *Deserts,* Karlheinz Stockhausen's *Gesang der Junglinge,* and Otto Luening's and Vladimir Ussachevsky's *Rhapsodic Variations, Poem for Cycles and Bells,* and *Concerted Piece for Tape Recorder and Orchestra.* As the latter title indicates, some of this music is dependent for its effects on the manipulation of electronic tape by means of repeating loops, running in reverse, splicing, filtering, and so on. Human and natural sounds also are used—wind, crowd noises, radios blaring—to create what has been called *musique concrète*—concrète music.

Stockhausen has continued to compose tape-manipulated music, including *Mikrophonie I, Mikrophonie II,* and *Opus 1970.* And a later generation of composers, including Alvin Lucier (*I Am Sitting in a Room*), Terry Riley (*Music for the Gift* and *In C*) and Steve Reich (*Gonna Rain* and *Come Out*), has advanced the art several steps further.

Naturally, the bulk of tape-processed works cannot be performed during live performances, for they are dependent on hours of complex preparation in the laboratory. With the use of the synthesizer and allied instruments, however, live electronic sounds can be produced, and many new-music composers are writing music for these instruments. Some have written music for electronic instruments alone; others have combined electronic instruments with conventional instruments. For a taste of this music, listen to Bernard Xolotl's *Last Wave* or *Procession*, Wendy Carlos's *Sonic Seasonings* or *Digital Moonscapes*, or Donald Erb's *In No Strange Land*.

Since the elements of sound—frequency, wavelength, and so on—can all be created electronically, some advocates of electronic music have suggested that the day will come when traditional orchestras will be obsolete, and all music will be created in the laboratory. More common is the belief that electronic instruments and techniques will simply take their places alongside more conventional modes of musical expression, providing the composer with a set of rich new resources to turn to when the occasion demands.

Minimalism

An exception to the rule that new music is difficult to listen to and places exceptional demands on the listener is provided by the major movement in serious music of the past two decades, *minimalism*. Much "minimal" music is melodic, and some of it is quite beautiful. The major composers of minimal music, Philip Glass, Steve Reich, Terry Riley, and La Monte Young foremost among them, wanted to simplify, to pare music down to its essential elements. As a result, much of what they have produced consists of bare fragments of music, simple harmonies, elementary patterns of melody and rhythm repeated over and over again. After extensive repetitions of the pattern it is altered slightly, and then the new pattern is repeated. Compared with most new music, which is dense, complex, and often confusing, minimal music seems simple and clear. The sound is familiar, but you may find yourself wondering, "Why all the repetition?" Listen to Steve Reich's *Sextet, Six Marimbas, Drumming,* or *Four Organs*; or Philip Glass's *Strung Out, Glassworks, Dance 1 and 3,* or *Company.* Listen to the music as pure sound, slowly and fantastically evolving like a living creature. Most music flies by us so fast we haven't a chance to thoroughly explore it. Minimalist music is music you can listen to down to the tiniest detail, examining each tone, chord, and rhythm as closely as you like.

Free Jazz

Paralleling all of these developments in classical music during the past two decades has been an explosion in the sound of jazz. While the means are quite different, the goal is the same: to find new modes of expression through the exploration of new sounds. New music in jazz began in 1958 with the work of saxophonist Ornette Coleman. Before that, jazz musicians had improvised their melodies freely, but always in relation to an underlying chord structure. As composers before Schönberg has based their compositions on a strong tonal foundation, so pre-Coleman jazz musicians based their improvisations on a pattern of strict chord changes.

Coleman began working on a new and totally free way of playing, one that was not dependent on chord changes. He found a few musicians interested in his ideas, and taught them to play without reference to the set patterns they had depended on in the past. At first, "No one knew where to go or what to do to show that he knew where he was going," Coleman has recalled, illustrating the difficulties he was up against. Slowly he taught the others to express themselves in a new and free way—to let the music evolve naturally without any preconceived notions of where it was going to go.

The freedom that Coleman sought soon became the goal of others, and the wild, explosive sound of new jazz was born. To this day it has not been adopted by most jazz musicians, who continue to play in a conventional style based on traditional chord sequences. To understand the difference, listen to the conventional jazz sounds of Miles Davis, the Modern Jazz Quartet, Stan Getz, Wynton Marsalis, Art Blakey, or Horace Silver. Compare these with a "free jazz" performer—Coleman, Archie Shepp, John Coltrane, Cecil Taylor, Albert Ayler, or Don Cherry, for example. With the latter, don't expect to be able to find your way easily. The music can be wild, frenzied, characterized by utter abandon by the musicians. But the energy, the virtuosity, and above all the passion and emotion of the music can make the experience of new jazz enormously rewarding.

Now on to the Next Step

If music history has taught us anything, it is that new music always becomes newer music. Just what the next steps in the evolution of classical music, jazz, and other forms of music will be, no one can say. All we know is that there *will* be next steps. Following them during the years ahead will be an exciting experience for every serious listener.

For an altogether different experience, try listening to some of the music of other cultures. Non-Western music has received very little attention in this book, but that does not mean it is not worthy of your attention. An endless variety of rich and rewarding music awaits you in the ethnic traditions of India, the Far East and Middle East, Africa, and Latin America. No special skills beyond those you have already learned are needed for you to find enjoyment in this music. An added benefit is that an attraction to the music of another country can lead you to an interest in the country itself, and a desire to study its history, art, and culture.

But don't stop there. Seek continually to widen your music horizons. Consider taking up a musical instrument if you haven't already, or singing in a choir or chorus. As a listener, delve into other eras, other forms of music, other modes of musical expression. Listen actively, avoiding the pitfalls of "easy listening," which pretend, nonsensically, that by relaxing and letting the music "flow," you can understand it. Even as an active, inquiring listener, you won't understand everything you listen to, for no one does, but you'll be expanding your boundaries continually. That, finally, is the goal of listening—and the key to understanding.

STUDY ACTIVITIES

1. Some computers are being programmed to write music. So far no masterpieces have resulted, but computer engineers never give up easily. Do you think a computer will ever write a great piece of music? Why or why not?
2. Is John Cage's *4′33″* music? Why or why not?
3. Suppose a chicken were to peck at the keys of a piano, thereby producing sounds. Would this be music? Why or why not?
4. Do you think that composers have a responsibility to write music that audiences will enjoy?
5. Choose an art form besides music that you are familiar with—art, dance, or literature, for example. During the past several decades, has the art form seen a gap between creator and audience open up, one similiar to the gap between composer and audience discussed in this chapter?

Glossary

The words defined here include terms from the text as well as terms a student might encounter in general readings on music.

Abstract music—Music which is free from references to events and experiences existing outside of music; distinguished from "program music."

Accent—Special emphasis on a single note or chord.

Accompaniment—A musical background supporting a soloist or an important melody.

Acoustics—The science of sound.

Ad lib—To improvise.

Allegro—A fast tempo; also used as the title of a movement in fast tempo.

Alto—The second highest part in choral music. The alto part lies between the soprano (highest) and the tenor (third highest).

Amplitude—The height of a wave. Amplitude determines the intensity (loudness or softness) of a sound.

Andante—A moderate tempo, slower than allegro but faster than largo; also used as the title of a movement in moderate tempo.

Aria—A difficult composition for solo voice with orchestral accompaniment.

Ars nova—Type of music written during the fourteenth and early fifteenth centuries. Roughly speaking, the Ars Nova period formed a connecting link between the late Medieval period and the early Renaissance.

Atonal—Music without a tonal center.

Baroque—Type of music written during the seventeenth and first half of the eighteenth centuries.

Bass—The lowest part in choral music. Also any very low sound.

Beat—The steady pulse which supports the rhythmic background in a piece of music.

Blues—A song in strophic form and based on a harmonic pattern of three repeating triads. The verses of most blues are 12 measures in length. Verses, usually telling of some hardship suffered by the performer, are often improvised.

Bop—Type of jazz popular for about 10 years beginning in the early 1940's. Bop was characterized by intricate improvisations based on extremely complex chord patterns. Leading bop performers included Charlie Parker (alto saxophone), Dizzy Gillespie (trumpet), and Thelonius Monk (piano).

Bowing—Causing a string to vibrate by drawing a bow across it. The bow consists of horsehair stretched tightly on a wooden stick.

Brass—Section of the orchestra consisting of French horns, tubas, trumpets, and trombones. Other brass instruments include the cornet, the baritone, and the Sousaphone.

Bridge—A section of music leading from one principal theme to another.

Cadenza—An improvised section near the end of a concerto or aria. The purpose of the cadenza is to give the performer an opportunity to display his technical skill.

Chamber music—Instrumental music where each part is played by one, and only one, performer. Chamber music is usually written for from two to eight performers. Common chamber music forms include the string quartet, the string trio, and the piano quartet.

Chord—Three or more notes played simultaneously.

Classical music—1. Music composed during the years 1750 to approximately 1820. The Classical period is generally thought of as lying between the Baroque period and the Romantic period of music history. 2. More generally, classical music refers to any music which is meant to be distinguished from "popular" music and its associated forms, such as jazz, rock, musical comedy, soul, etc.

Coda—A short section of new musical material placed at the end of a movement or a popular song.

Color—The quality of the sound produced by an instrument. Color helps us to distinguish between two instruments playing the same note at the same volume. Color arises from overtones produced by each instrument.

Composition—A complete musical work.

Concerto—An orchestral composition for a solo instrument, such as piano or violin, with orchestral accompaniment.

Consonant—Having a pleasing sound.

Content—The meaning and feeling contained in a musical composition.

Cycle—A fluctuation on a sound wave. The number of cycles occurring every second determines the frequency of the wave.

Development—The section of a composition written in sonata form in which the two principal themes are expanded upon.

Dissonant—Having an unpleasant sound.

Duple meter—(*see* Meter)

Electronic music—Music in which the sound waves are produced by electronic equipment such as photoelectric cells, computers, and synthesizers.

Exposition—The first section of a composition written in sonata form. In the exposition, the two principal themes are introduced.

Expressionistic—A type of music written during the early twentieth century characterized by sharp, angular melodies and harsh, clashing harmonies. Expressionistic music was highly emotional, the result of composers' attempts to sincerely express their inner feelings.

Folk song—A song of unknown authorship which is handed down from generation to generation until it becomes widely known among the people of a particular region.

Form—The organizing scheme which determines the structure of a piece of music.

Free jazz—A style of jazz created by Ornette Coleman, based on free improvisation without reference to an agreed-upon set of chord changes.

Frequency—The number of cycles occurring each second on a sound wave.

Fundamental—The frequency which the ear hears and identifies; to be distinguished from the higher frequencies (overtones) of a sound wave.

Gebrauchsmusik—Type of music written during the 1920's and 1930's and meant to serve a practical purpose. Thus, much of it was intended to be used informally by amateurs.

Harmony—The manner in which two or more melodies interact with each other.

Homophonic—Music which consists of a single melodic line supported by chords.

Hymn—A religious song, written to praise God.

Improvise—To create music spontaneously while playing for an audience.

Impressionistic—A type of music written during the late nineteenth and early twentieth centuries, characterized by soft, lyrical melodies and lush, shimmering harmonies. Impressionistic composers were interested in delicate beauty rather than harsh reality.

Instrumentation—(*see* Orchestration)

Jazz—A style of music developed in the United States during the early twentieth century. The chief characteristics of jazz are its use of improvised melodies and an easily recognizable beat.

Largo—A slow tempo; also used as the title of a movement in slow tempo.

Leitmotiv—A short melody used in Richard Wagner's operas. *Leitmotivs* were meant to be associated with particular characters, objects, or ideas.

Lyrical—Having a smooth, singing quality.

Lyrics—The words of a song.

Measure—A group of beats. Thus, a composition in duple meter will be divided into measures each containing two or four beats; a composition in triple meter will be divided into measures each containing three beats. Similarly for quintuple meter, etc.

Melody—The succession of notes which stands out above the rest of the music; the "tune."

Meter—The characteristic grouping of beats in a musical composition. A work in "duple" meter will be divided into small groups of two or four beats each. A work in "triple" meter will be divided into small groups of three beats each. A work in "quintuple" meter will be divided into small groups of five beats each.

Micro tone—An interval between musical tones that is smaller than a half-step.

Minimalism—A style of music developed during the 1960's which pares music down to its simplest melodies, rhythms, and harmonies.

Minuet—A stately dance of the seventeenth and eighteenth centuries. Most of the symphonies of Haydn and Mozart contained music for the minuet as their third movements.

Movement—One of the large subdivisions of a musical composition. Symphonies usually consist of four movements, while concertos normally have only three.

Musical comedy—A theatrical form developed in the United States during the first few decades of the twentieth century. The prime ingredients of a musical comedy are popular music, humor, drama, and dance.

Musique concrète—A style of music developed in the 1950's which uses tape recordings of sounds and noises as the materials for building music. The sounds of traditional musical instruments are avoided.

Neo-classical—A style of twentieth-century music which attempts to imitate the forms and ideals of the eighteenth century.

Note—A sound unchanging in frequency, produced by a single voice or musical instrument.

Octave—A note with twice the frequency of a given note. The two notes have the quality of sounding nearly identical, the only obvious difference being that one note is higher than the other.

Orchestration—The manner in which musical instruments are used in a composition; same as "instrumentation."

Opera—A drama in which all of the dialogue is sung to the accompaniment of an orchestra.

Operetta—An opera intended for a wide audience. To achieve this end, some of opera's traditional rules are relaxed. Thus, an operetta may contain spoken dialogue and popular music.

Overtone—A note corresponding to an integral multiple of the fundamental of a musical note.

Percussion—Section of the orchestra consisting of instruments whose sound is produced by vibrating in some manner a stretched skin or a solid object. Examples of percussion instruments include all of the drums, the xylophone, the cymbals, and the castanets.

Piano quartet—A composition for four instruments—piano, violin, viola, and cello.

Pitch—The highness or lowness of a musical note. The pitch is determined by the frequency of the note.

Pizzicato—Producing sound from a stringed instrument by plucking the strings.

Polyphonic—Music which consists of two or more independent melodic lines.

Polyrhythmic—Music which consists of melodies written in different meters sounding simultaneously.

Program music—Compositions attempting to depict events and experiences which lie outside music.

Pure sound—A sound having no overtones. Generally speaking, the fewer overtones a sound has, the purer it is considered to be.

Quintuple meter—(*see* Meter.)

Ragtime—A style of solo piano music popular at the turn of the century, characterized by a steady beat and sprightly, syncopated rhythms.

Recapitulation—The third section of a composition written in sonata form. The recapitulation consists of a re-statement of the two principal themes in their original forms.

Rest—An indication for an instrumentalist to stop playing temporarily.

Rhythm—The pattern of time-lengths set up by the individual notes of a melody.

Romantic—The period in music history extending roughly from 1820 to the early years of the twentieth century. Romantic music is characterized by the attempts of composers to translate into music the most passionate feelings of their souls.

Rondo—A musical form consisting of a single, unchanging section of musical material which alternates with a number of contrasting sections.

Rounded binary form—A musical form which follows an A A B A B A pattern.

Scale—A group of notes close to each other in frequency and arranged in ascending or descending order.

Solo—A performance by a single singer or instrumentalist.

Sonata—A composition in four movements for piano, or for a solo instrument with piano accompaniment.

Sonata form—The most important form of the Classical period in music history. A movement in sonata form consists of an exposition, a development, a recapitulation, and sometimes a coda.

Soprano—The highest part in choral music.

Staff—Five parallel horizontal lines on which notes are written to indicate music to be played or sung.

String quartet—A composition for four instruments—two violins, a viola, and a cello.

Strings—Section of the orchestra consisting of the violins, the violas, the cellos, and the double basses.

String trio—A composition for three stringed instruments. The most common combination is violin, viola, and cello.

Strophic form—A musical form in which the same music is repeated over and over again.

Swing—A type of jazz popularized by large dance bands in the 1930's. Among the most popular swing bands were those of Benny Goodman, Count Basie, and Chick Webb.

Symphony—A composition, generally in four movements, for the orchestra.

Syncopation—The use of accents in unpredictable places in a melody. Syncopation was an important characteristic of ragtime music as well as many early jazz compositions.

Tempo—The speed at which a musical composition is played.

Tenor—The third highest part in choral music. The tenor part lies between the alto (second highest) and the bass (lowest).

Ternary form—A composition in three sections, the third simply a repeat of the first. In letters, ternary form is diagrammed A B A.

Theme—An important melody.

Tonal center—A single keynote dictating the harmonic structure of a piece of music.

Tone color—(*see* Color)

Transitional music—Music which serves to connect two important sections of a piece of music.

Triad—The most common of all chords. The three notes of a triad can be produced by singing the second, third, and fourth words of *The Star-Spangled Banner.*

Trio—A composition for three instruments. The most common type is the piano trio, which utilizes a piano, a violin, and a cello.

Twelve-tone system—A system of composition devised by Arnold Schönberg which places equal emphasis on all of the 12 basic notes of music.

Triple meter—(*see* Meter)

Unison—Situation when two or more instruments or singers are producing the same note.

Variation form—A musical form consisting of a melody, its rhythm, and its harmony, followed by numerous variations of these three elements.

Waltz—A dance which first gained popularity at the beginnning of the nineteenth century. The waltz is characterized by the fact that it is always written in triple meter.

Wave—A vibration pattern which causes sound to be transmitted.

Woodwind—Section of the orchestra consisting of the flutes, clarinets, oboes, and saxophones.

Answers to Study Activity Questions

Chapter 1

2. b. The reasons that we like or dislike music are many and complex, relating to our tastes, values, and experience. If rock and roll music does not satisfy these reasons for someone who has listened to it diligently, that person probably won't like it.

   c. It may or may not, depending on how well rock and roll satisfies the reasons mentioned above.

3. He probably will not like all styles equally. He hasn't heard music, but assuming he has had a variety of experiences and has developed values and tastes in other areas of his life, he probably will find that certain styles of music satisfy him more than others.

5. See 2, b.

6. Don't make judgments about styles of music until, by diligent listening, you have given them a fair chance to prove themselves.

Chapter 2

3. The lyrics touch on many beautiful themes that may move us emotionally—home, lullabies, sleeping instead of crying. Most people will agree that the melody is indeed beautiful, but with lyrics like this, we might feel that even an ordinary, undistinguished melody was beautiful.

Chapter 3

1. Percussion instruments such as drums, wood blocks, and cymbals do not produce melodies, but they serve a very important role in creating rhythms in music.

5. You probably would not have enjoyed the piece less. But knowledge of the components of music—in this case, the meter—is always important in furthering our understanding and, ultimately, our enjoyment of that music.

Chapter 4

1. Melody 1: A B C D E F G
   Melody 2: H I J K L M N
   Melody 3: O P Q R S N U

2. a. Vertical
   b. Horizontal
   c. Vertical
   d. Vertical
   e. Horizontal
   f. Vertical
   g. Horizontal

3. A chord might sound dissonant because a person has been told it is an unpleasant sound, or has observed someone grimacing at the sound of the chord. Or subconsciously the person may associate the sound with an unpleasant experience that occurred at an earlier time when the sound was heard. The most likely reason that it sounds dissonant, however, is that it is different from the sounds the person is accustomed to.

Chapter 5

1. The size and shape of the vocal chords and the larynx.

2. a. The tuba and the flute.
   b. The trumpet and the clarinet.
   c. The oboe.

3. The bulk of the sound of a scratch occurs at above 7,000 cycles per second. The filter eliminates this.

4. The strings differ in thickness and in composition.

5. a. Hammers strike strings, causing them to vibrate.
   b. Air blows across reeds, causing them to vibrate.
   c. Mallets strike wooden bars, causing them to vibrate.
   d. Air blows through pipes, causing reeds to vibrate.
   e. Fingers pluck strings, causing them to vibrate.
   f. Air is blown past the grass, causing it to vibrate.

6. Frequency of fourth overtone = 5 × 440 = 2,200 cycles per second.

7. Frequency of fifth overtone = 1,728 cycles per second
   Frequency of fundamental = 1/6 x 1,728 = 288 cycles per second.

Chapter 6

1. a. Rondo, strophic, and variation
   b. Rounded binary, rondo, and variation
   c. Sonata, strophic, and rondo
   d. Strophic, rondo, and sonata

2. Since the recapitulation repeats the main themes of the exposition, we could label sonata form as E E D E D E, which is precisely rounded binary form.

3. It is unlikely there will be themes, repetition of themes, or form to the music.

4. They would differ in form, speed, character, meter, and instrumentation.

Chapter 7

2. If the music were played without the lyrics, it is likely that many listeners would find content in the music, content that almost certainly will be different from the content suggested by the lyrics. Thus, the music itself can dictate the content.

Chapter 8

1. One, two, and three octaves above: 1,200, 2,400, and 4,800 vibrations per second.

   One, two, and three octaves below: 300, 150, and 75 vibrations per second.

2. Dividing by 2 six times in succession gives 31 vibrations per second.

3. 16

4. 4

5. 64

6. We are so familiar with the rhythm of the song that it is almost impossible to think of the song in a different way.

7. A more important word will be more easily heard by listeners if it is set to a longer note like a whole note; a less important word can be set to a rapid sixteenth or thirty-second note.